As Earth's faster-than-light spaceship hung in the void between galaxies, Arcot, Wade, Morey and Fuller could see below them, like a vast shining horizon, the mass of stars that formed their own island universe. Morey worked a moment with his slide rule, then said, "We made good time! Twenty-nine light years in ten seconds! Yet you had it on at only half power...."

Arcot pushed the control lever all the way to full power. The ship filled with the strain of flowing energy, and sparks snapped in the air of the control room as they raced at an inconceivable speed through the darkness of intergalactic space.

But suddenly, far off to their left and far to their right, they saw two shining ships paralleling their course! They held grimly to the course of the Earth ship, bracketing it like an official guard.

The Earth scientists stared at them in wonder. "Lord," muttered Morey, "where can they have come from?"

JOHN W. CAMPBELL first started writing in 1930 when his first short story, *When the Atoms Failed,* was accepted by a science-fiction magazine. At that time he was twenty years old and still a student at college. As the title of the story indicates, he was even at that time occupied with the significance of atomic energy and nuclear physics.

For the next seven years, Campbell, bolstered by a scientific background that ran from childhood experiments, to study at Duke University and the Massachusetts Institute of Technology, wrote and sold science-fiction, achieving for himself an enviable reputation in the field.

In 1937 he became the editor of *Astounding Stories* magazine and applied himself at once to the task of bettering the magazine and the field of s-f writing in general. His influence on science-fiction since then has been great. Today he still remains as the editor of that magazine's evolved and redesigned successor, *Analog.*

ISLANDS
OF
SPACE

by

JOHN W. CAMPBELL

WILDSIDE PRESS

PROLOGUE

IN THE EARLY PART OF THE Twenty Second Century, Dr. Richard Arcot, hailed as "the greatest living physicist", and Robert Morey, his brilliant mathematical assistant, discovered the so-called "molecular motion drive", which utilized the random energy of heat to produce useful motion.

John Fuller, designing engineer, helped the two men to build a ship which used the drive in order to have a weapon to seek out and capture the mysterious Air Pirate whose robberies were ruining Transcontinental Airways.

The Pirate, Wade, was a brilliant but neurotic chemist who had discovered, among other things, the secret of invisibility. Cured of his instability by modern psychomedical techniques, he was hired by Arcot to help build an interplanetary vessel to go to Venus.

The Venusians proved to be a humanoid race of people who used telepathy for communication. Although they were similar to Earthmen, their blue blood and double thumbs made them enough different to have caused distrust and racial friction, had not both planets been drawn together in a common bond of defense by the passing of the Black Star.

The Black Star, Nigra, was a dead, burned-out sun surrounded by a planetary system very much like our own. But these people had been forced to use their science to produce enough heat and light to stay alive in the cold, black depths of interstellar space. There was nothing evil or menacing in their attack on the Solar System; they simply wanted a star that gave off light and heat. So they attacked, not realizing that they were attacking beings equal in intelligence to themselves.

They were at another disadvantage, too. The Nigrans had spent long millenia fighting their environment and had had no time to fight among themselves, so they knew nothing of how to wage a war. The Earthmen and Venusians knew only too well, since they had a long history of war on each planet.

Inevitably, the Nigrans were driven back to the Black Star.*

The war was over. And things became dull. And the taste of adventure still remained on the tongues of Arcot, Wade, and Morey.

---

*See *The Black Star Passes*, Ace Books, F-346.

I

THREE MEN sat around a table which was littered with graphs, sketches of mathematical functions, and books of tensor formulae. Beside the table stood a Munson-Bradley intergraph calculator which one of the men was using to check some of the equations he had already derived. The results they were getting seemed to indicate something well above and beyond what they had expected.

And anything that surprised the team of Arcot, Wade, and Morey was surprising indeed.

The intercom buzzed, interrupting their work.

Dr. Richard Arcot reached over and lifted the switch. "Arcot speaking."

The face that flashed on the screen was businesslike and

determined. "Dr. Arcot, Mr. Fuller is here. My orders are to check with you on all visitors."

Arcot nodded. "Send him up. But from now on, I'm not in to anyone but my father or the Interplanetary Chairman or the elder Mr. Morey. If they come, don't bother to call, just send 'em up. I will not receive calls for the next ten hours. Got it?"

"You won't be bothered, Dr. Arcot."

Arcot cut the circuit and the image collapsed.

Less than two minutes later, a light flashed above the door. Arcot touched the release, and the door slid aside. He looked at the man entering and said, with mock coldness:

"If it isn't the late John Fuller. What did you do—take a plane? It took you an hour to get here from Chicago."

Fuller shook his head sadly. "Most of the time was spent in getting past your guards. Getting to the seventy-fourth floor of the Transcontinental Airways Building is harder than stealing the Taj Mahal." Trying to suppress a grin, Fuller bowed low. "Besides, I think it would do your royal highness good to be kept waiting for a while. You're paid a couple of million a year to putter around in a lab while honest people work for a living. Then, if you happen to stub your toe over some useful gadget, they increase your pay. They call you scientists and spend the resources of two worlds to get you anything you want—and apologize if they don't get it within twenty-four hours.

"No doubt about it; it will do your majesties good to wait."

With a superior smile, he seated himself at the table and shuffled calmly through the sheets of equations before him.

Arcot and Wade were laughing, but not Robert Morey. With a sorrowful expression, he walked to the window and looked out at the hundreds of slim, graceful aircars that floated above the city.

"My friends," said Morey, almost tearfully, "I give you the great Dr. Arcot. These countless machines we see have come from one idea of his. Just an idea, mind you! And

8

who worked it into mathematical form and made it calculable, and therefore useful? I did!

"And who worked out the math for the interplanetary ships? I did! Without me they would never have been built!" He turned dramatically, as though he were playing King Lear. "And what do I get for it?" He pointed an accusing finger at Arcot. "What do I get? *He* is called 'Earth's most brilliant physicist', and I, who did all the hard work, am referred to as 'his mathematical assistant'." He shook his head solemnly. "It's a hard world."

At the table, Wade frowned, then looked at the ceiling. "If you'd make your quotations more accurate, they'd be more trustworthy. The news said that Arcot was the '*System's* most brilliant physicist', and that you were the brilliant mathematical assistant who showed great genius in developing the mathematics of Dr. Arcot's new theory'." Having delivered his speech, Wade began stoking his pipe.

Fuller tapped his fingers on the table. "Come on, you clowns, knock it off and tell me why you called a hard-working man away from his drafting table to come up to this play room of yours. What have you got up your sleeve this time?"

"Oh, that's too bad," said Arcot, leaning back comfortably in his chair. "We're sorry you're so busy. We were thinking of going out to see what Antares, Betelguese, or Polaris looked like at close range. And, if we don't get too bored, we might run over to the giant model nebula in Andromeda, or one of the others. Tough about your being busy; you might have helped us by designing the ship and earned your board and passage. Tough." Arcot looked at Fuller sadly.

Fuller's eyes narrowed. He knew Arcot was kidding, but he also knew how far Arcot would go when he was kidding —and this sounded like he meant it. Fuller said: "Look, teacher, a man named Einstein said that the velocity of light was tops over two hundred years ago, and nobody's come up with any counter evidence yet. Has the Lord instituted a new speed law?"

"Oh, no," said Wade, waving his pipe in a grand gesture of importance. "Arcot just decided he didn't like that law and made a new one himself."

"Now *wait* a minute!" said Fuller. "The velocity of light is a property of space!"

Arcot's bantering smile was gone. "Now you've got it, Fuller. The velocity of light, just as Einstein said, is a property of space. What happens if we change space?"

Fuller blinked. "Change space? How?"

Arcot pointed toward a glass of water sitting nearby. "Why do things look distorted through the water? Because the light rays are bent. Why are they bent? Because as each wave front moves from air to water, *it slows down.* The electromagnetic and gravitational fields between those atoms are strong enough to increase the curvature of the space between them. Now, what happens if we reverse that effect?"

"Oh," said Fuller softly. "I get it. By changing the curvature of the space surrounding you, you could get any velocity you wanted. But what about acceleration? It would take years to reach those velocities at any acceleration a man could stand."

Arcot shook his head. "Take a look at the glass of water again. What happens when the light comes *out* of the water? It speeds up again *instantaneously.* By changing the space around a spaceship, you instantaneously change the velocity of the ship to a comparable velocity in that space. And since every particle is accelerated at the same rate, you wouldn't feel it, any more than you'd feel the acceleration due to gravity in free fall."

Fuller nodded slowly. Then, suddenly, a light gleamed in his eyes. "I suppose you've figured out where you're going to get the energy to power a ship like that?"

"He has," said Morey. "Uncle Arcot isn't the type to forget a little detail like that."

"Okay, give," said Fuller.

Arcot grinned and lit up his own pipe, joining Wade in an attempt to fill the room with impenetrable fog.

"All right," Arcot began, "we needed two things: a tremendous source of power and a way to store it.

"For the first, ordinary atomic energy wouldn't do. It's not controllable enough and uranium isn't something we could carry by the ton. So I began working with high-density currents.

"At the temperature of liquid helium, near absolute zero, lead becomes a nearly perfect conductor. Back in nineteen twenty, physicists had succeeded in making a current flow for four hours in a closed circuit. It was just a ring of lead, but the resistance was so low that the current kept on flowing. They even managed to get six hundred amperes through a piece of lead wire no bigger than a pencil lead.

"I don't know why they didn't go on from there, but they didn't. Possibly it was because they didn't have the insulation necessary to keep down the corona effect; in a high-density current, the electrons tend to push each other sideways out of the wire.

"At any rate, I tried it, using *lux* metal as an insulator around the wire."

"Hold it!" Fuller interrupted. "What, may I ask, is *lux* metal?"

"That was Wade's idea," Arcot grinned. "You remember those two substances we found in the Nigran ships during the war?"

"Sure," said Fuller. "One was transparent and the other was a perfect reflector. You said they were made of light—photons so greatly condensed that they were held together by their gravitational fields."

"Right. We called them light-metal. But Wade said that was too confusing. With a specific gravity of 103.5, light-metal was certainly not a light metal! So Wade coined a couple of words. *Lux* is the Latin for light, so he named the transparent one *lux* and the reflecting one *relux*."

"It sounds peculiar," Fuller observed, "but so does every coined word when you first hear it. Go on with your story."

Arcot relit his pipe and went on. "I put a current of ten thousand amps through a little piece of lead wire, and

11

that gave me a current density of 10^{10} amps per square inch.

"Then I started jacking up the voltage, and modified the thing with a double-polarity field somewhat similar to the molecular motion field except that it works on a subnucleonic level. As a result, about half of the lead fed into the chamber became contraterrene lead! The atoms just turned themselves inside out, so to speak, giving us an atom with positrons circling a negatively charged nucleus. It even gave the neutrons a reverse spin, converting them into antineutrons.

"Result: total annihilation of matter! When the contraterrene lead atoms met the terrene lead atoms, mutual annihilation resulted, giving us pure energy.

"Some of this power can be bled off to power the mechanism itself; the rest is useful energy. We've got all the power we need—power, literally by the ton."

Fuller said nothing; he just looked dazed. He was well beginning to believe that these three men could do the impossible and do it to order.

"The second thing," Arcot continued, "was, as I said, a way to store the energy so that it could be released as rapidly or as slowly as we needed it.

"That was Morey's baby. He figured it would be possible to use the space-strain apparatus to store energy. It's an old method; induction coils, condensers, and even gravity itself are storing energy by straining space. But with Morey's apparatus we could store a lot more.

"A torus-shaped induction coil encloses all its magnetic field within it; the torus, or 'doughnut' coil, has a perfectly enclosed magnetic field. We built an enclosed coil, using Morey's principle, and expected to store a few watts of power in it to see how long we could hold it.

"Unfortunately, we made the mistake of connecting it to the city power lines, and it cost us a hundred and fifty dollars at a quarter of a cent per kilowatt hour. We blew fuses all over the place. After that, we used the relux plate generator.

"At any rate, the gadget can store power and plenty of it, and it can put it out the same way."

Arcot knocked the ashes out of his pipe and smiled at Fuller. "Those are the essentials of what we have to offer. We give you the job of figuring out the stresses and strains involved. We want a ship with a cruising radius of a thousand million light years."

"Yes, sir! Right away, sir! Do you want a gross or only a dozen?" Fuller asked sarcastically. "You sure believe in big orders! And whench cometh the cold cash for this lovely dream of yours?"

"That," said Morey darkly, "is where the trouble comes in. We have to convince Dad. As President of Transcontinental Airways, he's my boss, but the trouble is, he's also my father. When he hears that I want to go gallivanting off all over the Universe with you guys, he is very likely to turn thumbs down on the whole deal. Besides, Arcot's dad has a lot of influence around here, too, and I have a healthy hunch he won't like the idea, either."

"I rather fear he won't," agreed Arcot gloomily.

A silence hung over the room that felt almost as heavy as the pall of pipe smoke the air conditioners were trying frantically to disperse.

The elder Mr. Morey had full control of their finances. A ship that would cost easily hundreds of millions of dollars was well beyond anything the four men could get by themselves. Their inventions were the property of Transcontinental, but even if they had not been, not one of the four men would think of selling them to another company.

Finally, Wade said: "I think we'll stand a much better chance if we show them a big, spectacular exhibition; something really impressive. We'll point out all the advantages and uses of the apparatus. Then we'll show them complete plans for the ship. They might consent."

"They might," replied Morey smiling. "It's worth a try, anyway. And let's get out of the city to do it. We can go up to my place in Vermont. We can use the lab up there

13

for all we need. We've got everything worked out, so there's no need to stay here.

"Besides, I've got a lake up there in which we can indulge in a little atavism to the fish stage of evolution."

"Good enough," Arcot agreed, grinning broadly. "And we'll need that lake, too. Here in the city it's only eighty-five because the aircars are soaking up heat for their molecular drive, but out in the country it'll be in the nineties."

"To the mountains, then! Let's pack up!"

II

THE MANY BOOKS AND PAPERS they had collected were hastily put into the briefcases, and the four men took the elevator to the landing area on the roof.

"We'll take my car," Morey said. "The rest of you can just leave yours here. They'll be safe for a few days."

They all piled in as Morey slid into the driver's seat and turned on the power.

They rose slowly, looking below them at the traffic of the great city. New York had long since abandoned her rivers as trade routes; they had been covered solidly by steel decks which were used as public landing fields and ground car routes. Around them loomed titanic structures of glistening colored tile. The sunlight reflected brilliantly from them, and the contrasting colors of the buildings seemed to blend together into a great, multicolored painting.

The darting planes, the traffic of commerce down between the great buildings, and the pleasure cars above, combined to give a series of changing, darting shadows that wove a flickering pattern over the city. The long lines of ships coming in from Chicago, London, Buenos Aires and San Francisco, and the constant flow from across the Pole—from Russia, India, and China, were like mighty black serpents that wound their way into the city.

Morey cut into a Northbound traffic level, moved into the high-speed lane, and eased in on the accelerator. He held to the traffic pattern for two hundred and fifty miles, until he was well past Boston, then he turned at the first break and fired the ship toward their goal in Vermont.

Less than forty-five minutes since they had left New York, Morey was dropping the car toward the little mountain lake that offered them a place for seclusion. Gently, he let the ship glide smoothly into the shed where the first molecular motion ship had been ·built. Arcot jumped out, saying:

"We're here—unload and get going. I think a swim and some sleep is in order before we start work on this ship. We can begin tomorrow." He looked approvingly at the clear blue water of the little lake.

Wade climbed out and pushed Arcot to one side. "All right, out of the way, then, little one, and let a man get going." He headed for the house with the briefcases.

Arcot was six feet two and weighed close to two hundred, but Wade was another two inches taller and weighed a good fifty pounds more. His arms and chest were built on the same general plan as those of a gorilla. He had good reason to call Arcot little.

Morey, though still taller, was not as heavily formed, and weighed only a few pounds more than Arcot, while Fuller was a bit smaller than Arcot.

Due to several factors, the size of the average human being had been steadily increasing for several centuries. Only Wade would have been considered a "big" man by the average person, for the average man was over six feet tall.

They relaxed most of the afternoon, swimming and indulging in a few wrestling matches. At wrestling, Wade consistently proved himself not only built like a gorilla but muscled like one; but Arcot proved that skill was not without merit several times, for he had found that if he could make the match last more than two minutes, Wade's huge muscles would find an insufficient oxygen supply and tire quickly.

That evening, after dinner, Morey engaged Wade in a fierce battle of chess, with Fuller as an interested spectator. Arcot, too, was watching, but he was saying nothing.

After several minutes of uneventful play, Morey stopped suddenly and glared at the board. "Now why'd I make that move? I intended to move my queen over there to check your king on the red diagonal."

"Yeah," replied Wade gloomily, "that's what I wanted you to do. I had a sure checkmate in three moves."

Arcot smiled quietly.

They continued play for several moves, then it was Wade who remarked that something seemed to be influencing his play.

"I had intended to trade queens. I'm glad I didn't, though; I think this leaves me in a better position."

"It sure does," agreed Morey. "I was due to clean up on the queen trade. You surprised me, too; you usually go in for trades. I'm afraid my position is hopeless now."

It was. In the next ten moves, Wade spotted the weak points in every attack Morey made; the attack crumbled disastrously and white was forced to resign, his king in a hopeless position.

Wade rubbed his chin. "You know, Morey, I seemed to know exactly why you made every move, and I saw every possibility involved."

"Yeah—so I noticed," said Morey with a grin.

"Come on, Morey, let's try a game," said Fuller, sliding into the chair Wade had vacated.

Although ordinarily equally matched with Fuller, Morey again went down to disastrous defeat in an amazingly short time. It almost seemed as if Fuller could anticipate every move.

"Brother, am I off form today," he said, rising from the table. "Come on, Arcot—let's see you try Wade."

Arcot sat down, and although he had never played chess as extensively as the others, he proceeded to clean Wade out lock, stock, and barrel.

"Now what's come over you?" asked Morey in astonishment as he saw a very complicated formation working out, a formation he knew was far better than Arcot's usual game. He had just worked it out and felt very proud of it.

Arcot looked at him and smiled. "That's the answer, Morey!"

Morey blinked. "What—what's the answer to what?"

"Yes—I meant it—don't be so surprised—you've seen it done before. I have—no, not under him, but a more experienced teacher. I figured it would come in handy in our explorations."

Morey's face grew more and more astonished as Arcot's strange monologue continued.

Finally, Arcot turned to Wade, who was looking at him and Morey in wide-eyed wonder. And this time, it was Wade who began talking in a monologue.

"You *did?*" he said in a surprised voice. "When?" There was a long pause, during which Arcot stared at Wade with such intensity that Fuller began to understand what was happening.

"Well," said Wade, "if you've learned the trick so thoroughly, try it out. Let's see you project your thoughts! Go ahead!"

Fuller, now understanding fully what was going on, burst out laughing. "He *has* been projecting his thoughts! He hasn't said a word to you!" Then he looked at Arcot. "As a matter of fact, you've said so little that I don't know how you pulled this telepathic stunt—though I'm quite convinced that you did."

"I spent three months on Venus a while back," said Arcot, "studying with one of their foremost telepathists. Actually, most of that time was spent on theory; learning how to do it isn't a difficult proposition. It just takes practice.

17

"The whole secret is that everyone has the power; it's a very ancient power in the human brain, and most of the lower animals possess it to a greater degree than do humans. When Man developed language, it gave his thoughts more concreteness and permitted a freer and more clearly conceived type of thinking. The result was that telepathy fell into disuse.

"I'm going to show you how to do it because it will be invaluable if we meet a strange race. By projecting pictures and concepts, you can dispense with going to the trouble of learning the language.

"After you learn the basics, all you'll need is practice, but watch yourself! Too much practice can give you the great-granddaddy of all headaches! Okay, now to begin with . . ."

Arcot spent the rest of the evening teaching them the Venerian system of telepathy.

They all rose at nine. Arcot got up first, and the others found it expedient to follow his example shortly thereafter. He had brought a large Tesla coil into the bedroom from the lab and succeeded in inducing sufficient voltage in the bedsprings to make very effective, though harmless, sparks.

"Come on, boys, hit the deck! Wade, as chief chemist, you are to synthesize a little coffee and heat-treat a few eggs for us. We have work ahead today! Rise and shine!" He didn't shut off the coil until he was assured that each of them had gotten a considerable distance from his bed.

"Ouch!" yelled Morey. "Okay! Shut it off! I want to get my pants! We're all up! You win!"

After breakfast, they all went into the room they used as a calculating room. Here they had two different types of integraph calculators and plenty of paper and equipment to do their own calculations and draw graphs.

"To begin with," said Fuller, "let's decide what shape we want to use. As designer, I'd like to point out that a sphere is the strongest, a cube easiest to build, and a torpedo shape

18

the most efficient aerodynamically. However, we intend to use it in space, not air.

"And remember, we'll need it more as a home than as a ship during the greater part of the trip."

"We might need an aerodynamically stable hull," Wade interjected. "It came in mighty handy on Venus. They're darned useful in emergencies. What do you think, Arcot?"

"I favor the torpedo shape. Okay, now we've got a hull. How about some engines to run it? Let's get those, too. I'll name the general things first; facts and figures can come later.

"First: We must have a powerful mass-energy converter. We could use the cavity radiator and use cosmic rays to warm it, and drive the individual power units that way, or we can have a main electrical power unit and warm them all electrically. Now, which one would be the better?"

Morey frowned. "I think we'd be safer if we didn't depend on any one plant, but had each as separate as possible. I'm for the individual cavity radiators."

"Question," interjected Fuller. "How do these cavity radiators work?"

"They're built like a thermos bottle," Arcot explained. "The inner shell will be of rough relux, which will absorb the heat efficiently, while the outer one will be of polished relux to keep the radiation inside. Between the two we'll run a flow of helium at two tons per square inch pressure to carry the heat to the molecular motion apparatus. The neck of the bottle will contain the atomic generator."

Fuller still looked puzzled. "See here; with this new space strain drive, why do we have to have the molecular drive at all?"

"To move around near a heavy mass—in the presence of a strong gravitational field," Arcot said. "A gravitational field tends to warp space in such a way that the velocity of light is lower in its presence. Our drive tries to warp or strain space in the opposite manner. The two would simply cancel each other out and we'd waste a lot of power going nowhere. As a matter of fact, the gravitational field of the sun is so intense that we'll have to go out beyond the orbit of Pluto before we can use the space strain drive effectively."

"I catch," said Fuller. "Now to get back to the generators. I think the power units would be simpler if they were controlled from one electrical power source, and just as reliable. Anyway, the molecular motion power is controlled, of necessity, from a single generator, so if one is apt to go bad, the other is, too."

"Very good reasoning," smiled Morey, "but I'm still strong for decentralization. I suggest a compromise. We can have the main power unit and the main verticals, which will be the largest, controlled by individual cosmic ray heaters, and the rest run by electric power units. They'd be just heating coils surrounded by the field."

"A good idea," said Arcot. "I'm in favor of the compromise. Okay, Fuller? Okay. Now the next problem is weapons. I suggest we use a separate control panel and a separate generating panel for the power tubes we'll want in the molecular beam projectors."

The molecular beam projector simply projected the field that caused molecular motion to take place as wanted. As weapons, they were terrifically deadly. If half a mountain is suddenly thrown into the air because all the random motion of its molecules becomes concentrated in one direction, it becomes a difficult projectile to fight. Or touch the bow of a ship with the beam; the bow drops to absolute zero and is driven back on the stern, with all the speed of its billions of molecules. The general effect is similar to that produced by two ships having a head-on collision at ten miles per second.

Anything touched by the beam is broken by its own molecules, twisted by its own strength, and crushed by its own toughness. Nothing can resist it.

"My idea," Arcot went on, "was that since the same power is used for both the beams and the drive, we'll have two separate power-tube banks to generate it. That way, if one breaks down, we can switch to the other. We can even use both at once on the drive, if necessary; the molecular motion machines will stand it if we make them of relux and anchor them with lux metal beams. The projectors would be able to handle the power, too, using Dad's new system.

"That will give us more protection, and, at the same time, full power. Since we'll have several projectors, the power needed to operate the ship will be about equal to the power required to operate the projectors.

"And I also suggest we mount some heat beam projectors."

"Why?" objected Wade. "They're less effective than the molecular rays. The molecular beams are instantly irresistible, while the heat beams take time to heat up the target. Sure, they're unhealthy to deal with, but no more so than the molecular beam."

"True enough," Arcot agreed, "but the heat beam is more spectacular, and we may find that a mere spectacular display will accomplish as much as actual destruction. Besides, the heat beams are more local in effect. If we want to kill an enemy and spare his captive, we want a beam that will be deadly where it hits, not for fifty yards around."

"Hold it a second," said Fuller wearily. "Now it's heat beams. Don't you guys think you ought to explain a little bit to the poor goon who's designing this flying battlewagon? How did you get a heat beam?"

Arcot grinned. "Simple. We use a small atomic cavity radiator at one end of which is a rough relux parabolic filter. Beyond that is a lux metal lens. The relux heats up tremendously, and since there is no polished relux to reflect it back, the heat is radiated out through the lux metal lens as a powerful heat beam."

"Okay, fine," said Fuller. "But stop springing new gadgets on me, will you?"

"I'll try not to," Arcot laughed. "Anyway, let's get on to the main power plant. Remember that our condenser coil is a gadget for storing energy in space; we are therefore obliged to supply it with energy to store. Just forming the drive field alone will require two times ten to the twenty-

21

seventh ergs, or the energy of about *two and a half tons* of matter. That means a whale of a lot of lead wire will have to be fed into our conversion generators; it would take several hours to charge the coils. We'd better have two big chargers to do the job.

"The controls we can figure out later. How about it? Any suggestions?"

"Sounds okay to me," said Morey, and the others agreed.

"Good enough. Now, as far as air and water go, we can use the standard spacecraft apparatus, Fuller, so you can figure in any way you want to."

"We'll need a lab, too," Wade put in. "And a machine shop with plenty of spare parts—everything we can possibly think of. Remember, we may want to build some things out in space."

"Right. And I wonder—" Arcot looked thoughtful. "How about the invisibility apparatus? It may prove useful, and it won't cost much. Let's put that in, too."

The apparatus he mentioned was simply a high-frequency oscillator tube of extreme power which caused vibrations approaching light frequency to be set up in the molecules of the ship. As a result, the ship became transparent, since light could easily pass through the vibrating molecules.

There was only one difficulty; the ship was invisible, all right, but it became a radio sender and could easily be detected by a directional radio. However, if the secret were unknown, it was a very effective method of disappearing. And, since the frequency was so high, a special detector was required to pick it up.

"Is that all you need?" asked Fuller.

"Nope," said Arcot, leaning back in his chair. "Now comes the kicker. I suggest that we make the hull of foot-thick lux metal and line it on the inside with relux wherever we want it to be opaque. And we want relux shutters on the windows. Lux is too doggone transparent; if we came too close to a hot star, we'd be badly burned."

Fuller looked almost goggle-eyed. "A—*foot—of—lux!* Good

22

Lord, Arcot! This ship would weigh a quarter of a million tons! That stuff is *dense!*"

"Sure," agreed Arcot, "but we'll need the protection. With a ship like that, you could run through a planetoid without hurting the hull. We'll make the relux inner wall about an inch thick, with a vacuum between them for protection in a warm atmosphere. And if some tremendous force did manage to crack the outer wall, we wouldn't be left without protection."

"Okay, you're the boss," Fuller said resignedly. "It's going to have to be a big ship, though. I figure a length of about two hundred feet and a diameter of around thirty feet. The interior I'll furnish with aluminum; it'll be cheaper and lighter. How about an observatory?"

"Put it in the rear of the ship," Wade suggested. "We'll mount one of the Nigran telectroscopes."

"Control room in the bow, of course," Morey chipped in.

"I've got you," Fuller said. "I'll work the thing out and give you a cost estimate and drawings."

"Fine," said Arcot, standing up. "Meanwhile, the rest of us will work out our little exhibition to impress Mr. Morey and Dad. Come on, lads, let's get back to the lab."

III

IT WAS TWO WEEKS before Dr. Robert Arcot and his old friend Arthur Morey, president of Transcontinental Airways, were invited to see what their sons had been working on.

The demonstration was to take place in the radiation labs in the basements of the Transcontinental building. Arcot,

Wade, Morey, and Fuller had brought the equipment in from the country place in Vermont and set it up in one of the heavily-lined, vault-like chambers that were used for radiation experiments.

The two older men were seated before a huge eighty-inch three-dimensional television screen several floors above the level where the actual demonstration was going on.

"There can't be anyone in the room, because of radiation burns," explained Arcot, junior. "We could have surrounded the thing with relux, but then you couldn't have seen what's going on.

"I'm not going to explain anything beforehand; like magic, they'll be more astounding before the explanation is given."

He touched a switch. The cameras began to operate, and the screen sprang into life.

The screen showed a heavy table on which was mounted a small projector that looked something like a searchlight with several heavy cables running into it. In the path of the projector was a large lux metal crucible surrounded by a ring of relux, and a series of points of relux aimed into the crucible. These points and the ring were grounded. Inside the crucible was a small ingot of coronium, the strong, hard, Venerian metal which melted at twenty-five hundred degrees centigrade and boiled at better than four thousand. The crucible was entirely enclosed in a large lux metal case which was lined, on the side away from the projector, with roughened relux.

Arcot moved a switch on the control panel. Far below them, a heavy relay slammed home, and suddenly a solid beam of brilliant bluish light shot out from the projector, a beam so brilliant that the entire screen was lit by the intense glow, and the spectators thought that they could almost feel the heat.

It passed through the lux metal case and through the coronium bar, only to be cut off by the relux liner, which, since it was rough, absorbed over ninety-nine percent of the rays that struck it.

ISLANDS OF SPACE

The coronium bar glowed red, orange, yellow, and white in quick succession, then suddenly slumped into a molten mass in the bottom of the crucible.

The crucible was filled now with a mass of molten metal that glowed intensely white and seethed furiously. The slowly rising vapors told of the rapid boiling, and their settling showed that their temperature was too high to permit them to remain hot—the heat radiated away too fast.

For perhaps ten seconds this went on, then suddenly a new factor was added to the performance. There was a sudden crashing arc and a blaze of blue flame that swept in a cyclonic twisting motion inside the crucible. The blaze of the arc, the intense brilliance of the incandescent metal, and the weird light of the beam of radiation shifted in a fantastic play of colors. It made a strange and impressive scene.

Suddenly the relay sounded again; the beam of radiance disappeared as quickly as it had come. In an instant, the blue violet glare of the relux plate had subsided to an angry red. The violent arcing had stopped, and the metal was cooling rapidly. A heavy purplish vapor in the crucible condensed on the walls into black, flakey crystals.

The elder Arcot was watching the scene in the screen curiously. "I wonder—" he said slowly. "As a physicist, I should say it was impossible, but if it did happen, I should imagine these would be the results." He turned to look at Arcot junior. "Well, go on with your exhibition, son."

"I want to know your ideas when we're through, though, Dad," said the younger man. "The next on the program is a little more interesting, perhaps. At least it demonstrates a more commercial aspect of the thing."

The younger Morey was operating the controls of the handling robots. On the screen, a machine rolled in on caterpillar treads, picked up the lux case and its contents, and carried them off.

A minute later, it reappeared with a large electromagnet and a relux plate, to which were attached a huge pair of silver busbars. The relux plate was set in a stand directly in front of the projector, and the big electromagnet was set up directly behind the relux plate. The magnet leads were connected, and a coil, in the form of two toruses intersecting at right angles enclosed in a form-fitting relux case, had been connected to the heavy terminals of the relux plate. An ammeter and a heavy coil of coronium wire were connected in series with the coil, and a kilovoltmeter was connected across the terminals of the relux plate.

As soon as the connections were completed, the robot backed swiftly out of the room, and Arcot turned on the magnet and the ray projector. Instantly, there was a sharp deflection of the kilovoltmeter.

"I haven't yet closed the switch leading into the coil," he explained, "so there's no current." The ammeter needle hadn't moved.

Despite the fact that the voltmeter seemed to be shorted out by the relux plate, the needle pointed steadily at twenty-two. Arcot changed the current through the magnet, and the reading dropped to twenty.

The rays had been on at very low power, the air only slightly ionized, but as Arcot turned a rheostat, the intensity increased, and the air in the path of the beam shone with an intense blue. The relux plate, subject now to eddy currents, since there was no other path for the energy to take, began to heat up rapidly.

"I'm going to close the switch into the coil now," said Arcot. "Watch the meters."

A relay snapped, and instantly the ammeter jumped to read 4500 amperes. The voltmeter gave a slight kick, then remained steady. The heavy coronium spring grew warm and began to glow dully, while the ammeter dropped slightly because of the increased resistance. The relux plate cooled slightly, and the voltmeter remained steady.

"The coil you see is storing the energy that is flowing into it," Arcot explained. "Notice that the coronium resistor is increasing its resistance, but otherwise there is little increase in the back E.M.F. The energy is coming from the rays which strike the polarized relux plate to give the current."

He paused a moment to make slight adjustments in the controls, then turned his attention back to the screen.

The kilovoltmeter still read twenty.

"Forty-five hundred amperes at twenty thousand volts," the elder Arcot said softly. "Where is it going?"

"Take a look at the space within the right angle of the torus coils," said Arcot junior. "It's getting dark in there despite the powerful light shed by the ionized air."

Indeed, the space withing the twin coils was rapidly growing dark; it was darkening the image of the things behind it, oddly blurring their outlines. In a moment, the images were completely wiped out, and the region within the coils was filled with a strangely solid blackness.

"According to the instruments," young Arcot said, "we have stored fifteen thousand kilowatt hours of energy in that coil and there seems to be no limit to how much power we can get into it. Just from the power it contains, that coil is worth about forty dollars right now, figured at a quarter of a cent per kilowatt hour.

"I haven't been using anywhere near the power I can get out of this apparatus, either. Watch." He threw another switch which shorted around the coronium resistor and the ammeter, allowing the current to run into the coil directly from the plate.

"I don't have a direct reading on this," he explained, "but an indirect reading from the magnetic field in that room shows a current of nearly a *hundred million amperes!*"

The younger Morey had been watching a panel of meters on the other side of the screen. Suddenly, he shouted: "Cut it, Arcot! The conductors are setting up a secondary field in the plate and causing trouble."

Instantly, Arcot's hand went to a switch. A relay slammed open, and the ray projector died.

The power coil still held its field of enigmatic blackness.

"Watch this," Arcot instructed. Under his expert manipulation, a small robot handler rolled into the room. It had a pair of pliers clutched in one claw. The spectators watched the screen in fascination as the robot drew back its arm and hurled the pliers at the black field with all its might. The pliers struck the blackness and rebounded as if they had hit a rubber wall. Arcot caused the little machine to pick up the pliers and repeat the process.

Arcot grinned. "I've cut off the power to the coil. Unlike the ordinary induction coil, it isn't necessary to keep supplying power to the thing; it's a static condition.

"You can see for yourself how much energy it holds. It's a handy little gadget, isn't it?" He shut off the rest of the instruments and the television screen, then turned to his father.

"The demonstration is over. Got any theories, Dad?"

The elder Dr. Arcot frowned in thought. "The only thing I can think of that would produce an effect like that is a stream of positrons—or contraterrene nuclei. That would explain not only the heating, but the electrical display.

"As far as the coil goes, that's easy to understand. Any energy storage device stores energy the strain in space; here you can actually see the strain in space." Then he smiled at his son. "I see my ex-laboratory assistant has come a long way. You've achieved controlled, usable atomic energy through total annihilation of mass. Right?"

Arcot smiled back and nodded. "Right, Dad."

"Son, I wonder if you'd give me your data sheets on that process. I'd like to work out some of the mathematical problems involved."

"Sure, Dad. But right now—" Arcot turned toward the elder Mr. Morey. "—I'm more interested in the mathematics of finance. We have a proposition to put to you, Mr. Morey, and that proposition, simply stated, is—"

Perhaps it was simply stated, but it took fully an hour for Arcot, Wade, and Morey to discuss the science of it with the two older men, and Fuller spent another hour over the carefully drawn plans for the ship.

At last, the elder Mr. Morey settled back and looked vacantly at the ceiling. They were seated now in the conference room of Transcontinental Airways.

"Well, boys," said Mr. Morey, "as usual, I'm in a position where I'm forced to yield. I might refuse financial backing, but you could sell any one of those gadgets for close to a billion dollars and finance the expedition independently, or you could, with your names, request the money publicly and back it that way." He paused a moment. "I am, however, thinking more in terms of your safety than in terms of money." There was another long pause, then he smiled at the four younger men.

"I think, however, that we can trust you. Armed with cosmic and molecular rays, you should be able to put up a fair scrap anywhere. Also, I have never detected any signs of feeblemindedness in any of you; I don't think you'll get yourselves in a jam you can't get out of. I'll back you."

"I hate to interrupt your exuberance," said the elder Dr. Arcot, "but I should like to know the name of this remarkable ship."

"What?" asked Wade. "Name? Oh, it hasn't any."

The elder Morey shook his head sadly. "That is indeed an important oversight. If a crew of men can overlook so fundamental a thing, I wonder if they *are* to be trusted."

"Well, what are we going to call it, then?" asked Arcot.

"*Solarite II* might do," suggested Morey. "It will still be from the Solar System."

"I think we should be more broadminded," said Arcot. "We aren't going to stay in this system—not even in this galaxy. We might call it the *Galaxian.*"

"Did you say broadminded?" asked Wade. "Let's really be broad and call it the *Universite* or something like that. Or, better yet, call it *Flourine!* That's everywhere in the universe and the most active element there is. This ship will go everywhere in the universe and be the most active thing that ever existed!"

"A good name!" said the elder Morey. "That gets my vote!"

Young Arcot looked thoughtful. "That's mighty good—I like the idea—but it lacks ring." He paused, then, looking up at the ceiling, repeated slowly:

> *"Alone, alone, all, all alone;*
> *Alone on a wide, wide sea;*
> *Nor any saint took pity on*
> *My soul in agony."*

He rose and walked over to the window, looking out where the bright points of light that were the stars of space rode high in the deep violet of the moonlit sky.

"The sea of all space—the sea of vastness that lies between the far-flung nebulae—the mighty void—alone on a sea, the vastness of which no man can imagine—alone—alone where no other man has been; alone, so far from all matter, from all mankind, that not even light, racing at billions of miles each day, could reach home in less than a million years." Arcot stopped and stood looking out of the window.

Morey broke the silence. *"The Ancient Mariner."* He paused. " 'Alone' will certainly be right. I think that name takes all the prizes."

Fuller nodded slowly. "I certainly agree. *The Ancient Mariner.* It's kind of long, but it is *the* name."

It was adopted unanimously.

IV

THE ANCIENT MARINER was built in the big Transcontinental shops in Newark; the power they needed was not available in the smaller shops.

Working twenty-four hours a day, in three shifts, skilled men took two months to finish the hull according to Fuller's specifications. The huge walls of lux metal required great care in construction, for they could not be welded; they had to be formed in position. And they could only be polished under powerful magnets, where the dense magnetic field softened the lux metal enough to allow a diamond polisher to do the job.

When the hull was finished, there came the laborious work of installing the power plant and the tremendous power leads, the connectors, the circuits to the relays—a thousand complex circuits.

Much of it was standard: the molecular power tubes, the molecular ray projectors, the power tubes for the invisibility apparatus, and many other parts. All the relays were standard, the gyroscopic stabilizers were standard, and the electromagnetic braking equipment for the gyros was standard.

But there would be long days of work ahead for Arcot, Wade, and Morey, for only they could install the special equipment; only they could put in the complicated wiring, for no one else on Earth understood the circuits they had to establish.

During the weeks of waiting, Arcot and his friends worked on auxiliary devices to be used with the ship. They wanted to make some improvements on the old molecular ray pistols, and to develop atomic powered heat projectors for hand use. The primary power they stored in small space-strain coils in the handgrip of the pistol. Despite their small size, the coils were capable of storing power for thirty hours of continuous operation of the rays. The finished weapon was scarcely larger than a standard molecular ray pistol.

Arcot pointed out that many of the planets they might visit would be larger than Earth, and they lacked any way of getting about readily under high gravity. Since something had to be done about that, Arcot did it. He demonstrated it to his friends one day in the shop yard.

Morey and Wade had just been in to see Fuller about

some details of the ship, and as they came out, Arcot called them over to his work bench. He was wearing a space suit without the helmet.

The modern space suit is made of woven lux metal wires of extremely small diameter and airproofed with a rubberoid flurocarbon plastic, and furnished with air and heating units. Made as it was, it offered protection nothing else could offer; it was almost a perfect insulator and was resistant to the attack of any chemical reagent. Not even elemental flourine could corrode it. And the extreme strength of the lux metal fiber made it stronger, pound for pound, than steel or coronium.

On Arcot's back was a pack of relux plated metal. It was connected by relux web belts to a broad belt that circled Arcot's waist. One thin cable ran down the right arm to a small relux tube about eight inches long by two inches in diameter.

"Watch!" Arcot said, grinning.

He reached to his belt and flipped a little switch.

"So long! See you later!" He pointed his right arm toward the ceiling and sailed lightly into the air. He lowered the angle of his arm and moved smoothly across the huge hangar, floating toward the shining bulk of the rapidly forming *Ancient Mariner*. He circled the room, rising and sinking at will, then headed for the open door.

"Come out and watch me where there's more room," he called.

Out in the open, he darted high up into the air until he was a mere speck in the sky. Then he suddenly came dropping down and landed lightly before them, swaying on his feet and poised lightly on his toes.

"Some jump," said Morey, in mock surprise.

"Yeah," agreed Fuller. "Try again."

"Or," Wade put in, "give me that weight annihilator and I'll beat you at your own game. What's the secret?"

"That's a cute gadget. How much load does it carry?" asked Morey, more practically.

"I can develop about ten tons as far as it goes, but the

32

human body can't take more than five gravities, so we can only visit planets with less than that surface gravity. The principle is easy to see; I'll show you."

He unhooked the cables and took the power pack from his back. "The main thing is the molecular power unit here, electrically heated and mounted on a small, massive gyroscope. That gyro is necessary, too. I tried leaving it out and almost took a nosedive. I had it coupled directly to the body and leaned forward a little bit when I was in the air. Without a gyro to keep the drive upright, I took a loop and started heading for the ground. I had to do some fancy gymnastics to keep from ending up six feet under—literally.

"The power is all generated in the pack with a small power plate and several storage coils. I've also got it hooked to these holsters at my belt so we can charge the pistols while we carry them.

"The control is this secondary power cable running down my arm to my hand. That gives you your direction, and the rheostat here at the belt changes the velocity.

"I've only made this one so far, but I've ordered six others like it. I thought you guys might like one, too."

"I think you guessed right!" said Morey, looking inside the power case. "Hey! Why all the extra room in the case?"

"It's an unperfected invention as yet; we might want to put some more stuff in there for our own private use."

Each of the men tried out the apparatus and found it quite satisfactory.

Meanwhile, there was other work to be done.

Wade had been given the job of gathering the necessary food and anything else in the way of supplies that he might think of. Arcot was collecting the necessary spare parts and apparatus. Morey was gathering a small library and equipping a chemistry laboratory. Fuller was to get together the necessary standard equipment for the ship—tables, seats, bunks, and other furniture.

It took months of work, and it seemed it would never

be finished, but finally, one clear, warm day in August, the ship was completely equipped and ready to go.

On the last inspection, the elder Dr. Arcot and the elder Mr. Morey went with the four younger men. They stood beside the great intergalactic cruiser, looking up at its shining hull.

"We came a bit later than we expected, son," said Dr. Arcot, "but we still expect a good show." He paused and frowned. "I understand you don't intend to take any trial trip. What's the idea?"

Arcot had been afraid his father would be worried about that, so he framed his explanation carefully. "Dad, we figured this ship out to the last decimal place; it's the best we can make it. Remember, the molecular motion drive will get a trial first; we'll give it a trial trip when we leave the sun. If there's any trouble, naturally, we'll return. But the equipment is standard, so we're expecting no trouble.

"The only part that would require a trial trip is the space-control apparatus, and there's no way to give that a trial trip. Remember, we have to get far enough out from the sun so that the gravitational field will be weak enough for the drive to overcome it. If we tried it this close, we'd just be trying to neutralize the sun's gravity. We'd be pouring out energy, wasting a great deal of it; but out away from the sun, we'll get most of the energy back.

"On the other hand, when we do get out and get started we will go faster than light, and we'd be hopelessly beyond the range of the molecular motion drive in an instant. In other words, if the space-control drive doesn't work, we can't come back, and if it does work, there's no need to come back.

"And if anything goes wrong, we're the only ones who could fix it, anyway. If anything goes wrong, I'll radio Earth. You ought to be able to hear from me in about a dozen years." He smiled suddenly. "Say! We might go out and get back here in time to hear ourselves talking!

"But you can see why we felt that there was little reason

34

for a trial trip. If it's a failure, we'll never be back to say so; if it isn't, we'll be able to continue."

His father still looked worried, but he nodded in acquiescence. "Perfect logic, son, but I guess we may as well give up the discussion. Personally, I don't like it. Let's see this ship of yours."

The great hull was two hundred feet long and thirty feet in diameter. The outer wall, one foot of solid lux metal, was separated from the inner, one-inch relux wall by a two inch gap which would be evacuated in space. The two walls were joined in many places by small lux metal crossbraces. The windows consisted of spaces in the relux wall, allowing the occupants to see through the transparent lux hull.

From the outside, it was difficult to detect the exact outline of the ship, for the clear lux metal was practically invisible and the foot of it that surrounded the more visible part of the ship gave a curious optical illusion. The perfect reflecting ability of the relux made the inner hull difficult to see, too. It was more by absence than presence that one detected it; it blotted out things behind it.

The great window of the pilot room disclosed the pilot seats and the great switchboard to one side. Each of the windows was equipped with a relux shield that slid into position at the touch of a switch, and these were already in place over the observatory window, so only the long, narrow portholes showed the lighted interior.

For some minutes, the elder men stood looking at the graceful beauty of the ship.

"Come on in—see the inside," suggested Fuller.

They entered through the airlock close to the base of the ship. The heavy lux door was opened by automatic machinery from the inside, but the combination depended on the use of a molecular ray and the knowledge of the correct place, which made it impossible for anyone to open it unless they had the ray and knew where to use it.

From the airlock, they went directly to the power room. Here they heard the soft purring of a large oscillator tube and the indistinguishable murmur of smoothly running AC generators powered by large contraterrene reactors.

The elder Dr. Arcot glanced in surprise at the heavy-duty ammeter in a control panel.

"Half a billion amperes! Good Lord! Where is all that power going?" He looked at his son.

"Into the storage coils. It's going in at ten kilovolts, so that's a five billion kilowatt supply. It's been going for half an hour and has half an hour to run. It takes two tons of matter to charge the coil to capacity, and we're carrying twenty tons of fuel—enough for ten charges. We shouldn't need more than three tons if all goes well, but 'all' seldom does.

"See that large black cylinder up there?" Arcot asked, pointing.

Above them, lying along the roof of the power room, lay a great black cylinder nearly two feet in diameter and extending out through the wall in the rear. It was made integral with two giant lux metal beams that reached to the bow of the ship in a long, sweeping curve. From one of the power switchboards, two heavy cables ran up to the giant cylinder.

"That's the main horizontal power unit. We can develop an acceleration of ten gravities either forward or backward. In the curve of the ship, on top, sides, and bottom, there are power units for motion in the other two directions.

"Most of the rest of the stuff in this section is old hat to you, though. Come on into the next room."

Arcot opened the heavy relux door, leading the way into the next room, which was twice the size of the power room. The center of the floor was occupied by a heavy pedestal of lux metal upon which was a huge, relux-encased, double torus storage coil. There was a large switchboard at the opposite end, while around the room, in ordered groups, stood the familiar double coils, each five feet in diameter. The space within them was already darkening.

"Well," said Arcot, senior, "that's some battery of power

coils, considering the amount of energy one can store. But what's the big one for?"

"That's the main space control," the younger Arcot answered. "While our power is stored in the smaller ones, we can shoot it into this one, which, you will notice, is constructed slightly differently. Instead of holding the field within it, completely enclosed, the big one will affect all the space about it. We will then be enclosed in what might be called a hyperspace of our own making."

"I see," said his father. "You go into hyperspace and move at any speed you please. But how will you see where you're going?"

"We won't, as far as I know. I don't expect to see a thing while we're in that hyperspace. We'll simply aim the ship in the direction we want to go and then go into hyperspace. The only thing we have to avoid is stars; their gravitational fields would drain the energy out of the apparatus and we'd end up in the center of a white-hot star. Meteors and such, we don't have to worry about; their fields aren't strong enough to drain the coils, and since we won't be in normal space, we can't hit them."

The elder Morey looked worried. "If you can't see your way back you'll get lost! And you can't radio back for help."

"Worse that that!" said Arcot. "We couldn't receive a signal of any kind after we get more than three hundred light years away; there weren't any radios before that.

"What we'll do is locate ourselves through the sun's light. We'll take photographs every so often and orient ourselves by them when we come back."

"That sounds like an excellent method of stellar navigation," agreed Morey senior. "Let's see the rest of the ship." He turned and walked toward the farther door.

The next room was the laboratory. On one side of the room was a complete physics lab and on the other was a well-stocked and well-equipped chemistry lab. They could perform many experiments here that no man had been able to perform due to lack of power. In this ship they had more generating facilities than all the power stations of Earth combined!

Arcot opened the next door. "This next room is the physics and chemistry storeroom. Here we have a duplicate—in some cases, six or seven duplicates—of every piece of apparatus on board, and plenty of material to make more. Actually, we have enough equipment to make a new ship out of what we have here. It would be a good deal smaller, but it would work.

"The greater part of our materials is stored in the curvature of the ship, where it will be easy to get at if necessary. All our water and food is there, and the emergency oxygen tanks.

"Now let's take the stairway to the upper deck."

The upper deck was the main living quarters. There were several small rooms on each side of the corridor down the center; at the extreme nose was the control room, and at the extreme stern was the observatory. The observatory was equipped with a small but exceedingly powerful telectroscope, developed from those the Nigrans had left on one of the deserted planets Sol had captured in return for the loss of Pluto to the Black Star. The arc commanded by the instrument was not great, but it was easy to turn the ship about, and most of their observations could be made without trouble.

Each of the men had a room of his own; there was a small galley and a library equipped with all the books the four men could think of as being useful. The books and all other equipment were clamped in place to keep them from flying around loose when the ship accelerated.

The control room at the nose was surrounded by a hemisphere of transparent lux metal which enabled them to see in every direction except directly behind, and even that blind spot could be covered by stationing a man in the observatory.

There were heat projectors and molecular ray projectors, each operated from the control room in the nose. To complete the armament, there were more projectors in the stern, controlled from the observatory, and a set on either side controlled from the library and the galley.

The ship was provisioned for two years—two years without stops. With the possibility of stopping on other planets, the four men could exist indefinitely in the ship.

After the two older men had been shown all through the intergalactic vessel, the elder Arcot turned to his old friend. "Morey, it looks as if it was time for us to leave the *Ancient Mariner* to her pilots!"

"I guess you're right. Well—I'll just say goodbye—but you all know there's a lot more I could say." Morey senior looked at them and started toward the airlock.

"Goodbye, son," said the elder Arcot. "Goodbye, men. I'll be expecting you any time within two years. We can have no warning, I suppose; your ship will outrace the radio beam. Goodbye." Dr. Arcot joined his old friend and they went outside.

The heavy lux metal door slid into place behind them, and the thick plastic cushions sealed the entrance to the airlock.

The workmen and the other personnel around the ship cleared the area and stood well back from the great hull. The two older men waved to the men inside the ship.

Suddenly the ship trembled, and rose toward the sky.

V

ARCOT, AT THE CONTROLS of the *Ancient Mariner*, increased the acceleration as the ship speared up toward interplanetary space. Soon, the deep blue of the sky had given way to an intense violet, and this faded to the utter black of space as the ship drew away from the planet that was its home.

"That lump of dust there is going to look mighty little when we get back," said Wade softly.

"But," Arcot reminded him, "that little lump of dust is going to pull us across a distance that our imaginations can't conceive of. And we'll be darned happy to see that pale globe swinging in space when we get back—provided, of course, that we do get back."

The ship was straining forward now under the pull of its molecular motion power units, accelerating at a steady rate, rapidly increasing the distance between the ship and Earth.

The cosmic ray power generators were still charging the coils, preventing the use of the space strain drive. Indeed, it would be a good many hours before they would be far enough from the sun to throw the ship into hyperspace.

In the meantime, Morey was methodically checking every control as Arcot called out the readings on the control panel. Everything was working to perfection. Their every calculation had checked out in practice so far. But the real test was yet to come.

They were well beyond the orbit of Pluto when they decided they would be safe in using the space strain drive and throwing the ship into hyperspace.

Morey was in the hyperspace control room, watching the instruments there. They were ready!

"Hold on!" called Arcot. "Here we go—if at all!" He reached out to the control panel before him and touched the green switch that controlled the molecular motion machines. The big power tubes cut off, and their acceleration ceased. His fingers pushed a brilliant red switch—there was a dull, muffled thud as a huge relay snapped shut.

Suddenly, a strange tingling feeling of power ran through them—space around them was suddenly black. The lights dimmed for an instant as the titanic current that flowed through the gigantic conductors set up a terrific magnetic field, reacting with the absorption plates. The power seemed to climb rapidly to a maximum—then, quite suddenly, it was gone.

The ship was quiet. No one spoke. The meters, which had flashed over to their limits, had dropped back to zero once more, except those which indicated the power stored in the giant coil. The stars that had shone brilliantly around them in a myriad of colors were gone. The space around them glowed strangely, and there was a vast cloud of strange, violet or pale green stars before them. Directly ahead was one green star that glowed big and brilliant, then it faded rapidly and shrank to a tiny dot—a distant star. There was a strange tenseness about the men; they seemed held in an odd, compelled silence.

Arcot reached forward again. "Cutting off power, Morey!" The red tumbler snapped back. Again space seemed to be charged with a vast surplus of energy that rushed in from all around, coursing through their bodies, producing a tingling feeling. Then space rocked in a gray cloud about them; the stars leaped out at them in blazing glory again.

"Well, it worked once!" breathed Arcot with a sigh of relief. "Lord, I made some errors in calculation, though! I hope I didn't make any more! Morey—how was it? I only used one-sixteenth power."

"Well, don't use any more, then," said Morey. "We sure traveled! The things worked perfectly. By the way, it's a good thing we had all the relays magnetically shielded; the magnetic field down here was so strong that my pocket kit tried to start running circles around it.

"According to your magnetic drag meter, the conductors were carrying over fifty billion amperes. The small coils worked perfectly. They're charged again; the power went back into them from the big coil with only a five percent loss of power—about twenty thousand megawatts."

"Hey, Arcot," Wade said. "I thought you said we wouldn't be able to see the stars."

Arcot spread his hands. "I did say that, and all my apologies for it. But we're not seeing them by light. The stars all have projections—shadows—in this space because of their intense gravitational fields. There are probably slight fluctuations in the field, perhaps one every minute or so. Since we were approaching them at twenty thousand times the speed of light, the Doppler effect gives us what looks like violet light.

"We saw the stars in front of us as violet points. The green ones were actually behind us, and the green light was tremendously reduced in frequency. It certainly can't be anything less than gamma rays and probably even of greater frequency.

"Did you notice there were no stars off to the side? We weren't approaching them, so they didn't give either effect."

"How did you know which was which?" asked Fuller skeptically.

"Did you see that green star directly ahead of us?" Arcot asked. "The one that dwindled so rapidly? That could only have been the sun, since the sun was the only star close enough to show up as a disc. Since it was green and I knew it was behind us, I decided that all the green ones were behind us. It isn't proof, but it's a good indication."

"You win, as usual," admitted Fuller.

"Well, where are we?" asked Wade. "I think that's more important."

"I haven't the least idea," confessed Arcot. "Let's see if we can find out. I've got the robot pilot on, so we can leave the ship to itself. Let's take a look at Old Sol from a distance that no man ever reached before!"

They started for the observatory. Morey joined them and Arcot put the view of Sol and his family on the telectro-scope screen. He increased the magnification to maximum, and the four men looked eagerly at the system. The sun glowed brilliantly, and the planets showed plainly.

"Now, if we wanted to take the trouble, we could calculate when the planets were in that position and determine the distance we have come. However, I notice that Pluto is still in place, so that means we are seeing the Solar System as it was before the passing of the Black Star. We're at least two light years away."

42

"More than that," said Morey. He pointed at the screen. "See here, how Mars is placed in relation to Venus and Earth? The planets were in that configuration seven years ago. We're seven light years from Earth."

"Good enough!" Arcot grinned. "That means we're within two light years of Sirius, since we were headed in that direction. Let's turn the ship so we can take a look at it with the telectroscope."

Since the power had been cut off, the ship was in free fall, and the men were weightless. Arcot didn't try to walk toward the control room; he simply pushed against the wall with his feet and made a long, slow dive for his destination.

The others reached for the handgrips in the walls while Arcot swung the ship gently around so that its stern was pointed toward Sirius. Because of its brilliance and relative proximity to Sol, Sirius is the brightest star in the heavens, as seen from Earth. At this much lesser distance, it shone as a brilliant point of light that blazed wonderfully. They turned the telectroscope toward it, but there was little they could see that was not visible from the big observatory on the Moon.

"I think we may as well go nearer," suggested Morey, "and see what we find on close range observation. Meanwhile, turn the ship back around and I'll take some pictures of the sun and its surrounding star field from this distance. Our only way of getting back is going to be this series of pictures, so I think we had best make it complete. For the first light century, we ought to take a picture every ten light years, and after that one each light century until we reach a point where we are only getting diminishing pictures of the local star cluster. After that, we can wait until we reach the edge of the Galaxy."

"Sounds all right to me," agreed Arcot. "After all, you're the astronomer, I'm not. To tell you the truth, I'd have to search a while to find Old Sol again. I can't see just where he is. Of course, I could locate him by means of the gyroscope settings, but I'm afraid I wouldn't find him so easily visually."

"Say! You sure are a fine one to pilot an expedition in space!" cried Wade in mock horror. "I think we ought to demote him for that! Imagine! He plans a trip of a thousand million light years, and then gets us out seven light years and says he doesn't know where he is! Doesn't even know where home is! I'm glad we have a cautious man like Morey along." He shook his head sadly.

They took a series of six plates of the sun, using different magnifications.

"These plates will help prove our story, too," said Morey as he looked at the finished plates. "We might have gone only a little way into space, up from the plane of the ecliptic and taken plates through a wide angle camera. But we'd have had to go at least seven years into the past to get a picture like this."

The new self-developing short-exposure plates, while not in perfect color balance, were more desirable for this work, since they took less time on exposure.

Morey and the others joined Arcot in the control room and strapped themselves into the cushioned seats. Since the space strain mechanism had proved itself in the first test, they felt they needed no more observations than they could make from the control room meters.

Arcot gazed out at the spot that was their immediate goal and said slowly: "How much bigger than Sol is that star, Morey?"

"It all depends on how you measure size," Morey replied. "It is two and a half times as heavy, has four times the volume, and radiates twenty-five times as much light. In other words, one hundred million tons of matter disappear each second in that star.

"That's for Sirius A, of course. Sirius B, its companion, is a different matter; it's a white dwarf. It has only one one-hundred-twenty-five-thousandths the volume of Sirius A, but it weighs *one third* as much. It radiates more per square inch than our sun, but, due to its tiny size, it is very faint. That star, though almost as massive as the sun, is only about the size of Earth."

44

"You sure have those statistics down pat!" said Fuller, laughing. "But I must say they're interesting. What's that star made of, anyway? Solid lux metal?"

"Hardly!" Morey replied. "Lux metal has a density of around 103, while this star has a density so high that one cubic inch of its matter would weigh a ton on Earth."

"Wow!" Wade ejaculated. "I'd hate to drop a baseball on my toe on that star!"

"It wouldn't hurt you," Arcot said, smiling. "If you could lift the darned thing, you ought to be tough enough to stand dropping it on your toe. Remember, it would weigh about two hundred tons! Think you could handle it?"

"At any rate, here we go. When we get there, you can get out and try it."

Again came the shock of the start. The heavens seemed to reel about them; the bright spot of Sirius was a brilliant violet point that swelled like an expanding balloon, spreading out until it filled a large angle.

Then again the heavens reeled, and they were still. The control room was filled with a dazzling splendor of brilliant blue-white light, and an intense heat beat in upon them.

"Brother! Feel that heat," said Arcot in awe. "We'd better watch ourselves; that thing is giving off plenty of ultraviolet. We could end up with third-degree sunburns if we're not careful." Suddenly he stopped and looked around in surprise. "Hey! Morey! I thought you said this was a double star! Look over there! That's no white dwarf—*it's a planet!*"

"Ridiculous!" snapped Morey. "It's impossible for a planet to be in equilibrium about a double star! But—" He paused, bewildered. "But it is a planet! But—but it can't be! We've made too many measurements on this star to make it possible!"

"I don't give a hang whether it can or not," Wade said coolly, "the fact remains that it is. Looks as if that shoots a whole flock of holes in that bedtime story you were telling us about a superdense star."

"I make a motion we look more closely first," said Fuller, quite logically.

But at first the telectroscope only served to confuse them more. It was most certainly a planet, and they had a strange, vague feeling of having seen it before.

Arcot mentioned this, and Wade launched into a long, pedantic discussion of how the left and right hemispheres of the brain get out of step at times, causing a sensation of having seen a thing before when it was impossible to have seen it previously.

Arcot gave Wade a long, withering stare and then pushed himself into the library without saying a word. A moment later, he was back with a large volume entitled: *"The Astronomy of the Nigran Invasion,"* by *D. K. Harkness.* He opened the volume to a full-page photograph of the third planet of the Black Star as taken from a space cruiser circling the planet. Silently, he pointed to it and to the image swimming on the screen of the telectroscope.

"Good Lord!" said Wade in astonished surprise. "It's impossible! We came here faster than light, and that planet got here first!"

"As you so brilliantly remarked a moment ago," Arcot pointed out, "I don't give a hang whether it can or not—it is. How they did it, I don't know, but it does clear up a number of things. According to the records we found, the ancient Nigrans had a force ray that could move planets from their orbits. I wonder if it couldn't be used to break up a double star? Also, we know their scientists were looking for a method of moving faster than light; if we can do it, so could they. They just moved their whole system of planets over here after getting rid of the upsetting influence of the white dwarf."

"Perfect!" exclaimed Morey enthusiastically. "It explains everything."

"Except that we saw that companion star when we stopped back there, half an hour ago," said Fuller.

"Not half an hour ago," Arcot contradicted. "Two years ago. We saw the light that left the companion before it was moved. It's rather like traveling in time."

"If that's so," asked Fuller, suddenly worried, "what is our time in relation to Earth?"

"If we moved by the space-strain drive at all times," Arcot explained, "we would return at exactly the same time we left. Time is passing normally on Earth as it is with us right now, but whenever we use the space-strain, we move instantaneously from one point to another as far as Earth and the rest of the universe is concerned. It seems to take time to us because we are within the influence of the field.

"Suppose we were to take a trip that required a week. In other words, three days traveling in space-strain, a day to look at the destination, and three more days coming back. When we returned to Earth, they would insist we had only been gone one day, the time we spent out of the drive. See?"

"I catch," said Fuller. "By the way, shouldn't we take some photographs of this system? Otherwise, Earth won't get the news for several years yet."

"Right," agreed Morey. "And we might as well look for the other planets of the Black Star, too."

They made several plates, continuing their observations until all the planets had been located, even old Pluto, where crews of Nigran technicians were obviously at work, building giant structures of lux metal. The great cities of the Nigrans were beginning to bloom on the once bleak plains of the planet. The mighty blaze of Sirius had warmed Pluto, vaporizing its atmosphere and thawing its seas. The planet that the Black Star had stolen from the Solar System was warmer than it had been for two billion years.

"Well, that's it," said Arcot when they had finished taking the necessary photographs. "We can prove we went faster than light easily, now. The astronomers can take up the work of classifying the planets and getting details of the orbits when we get back.

"Since the Nigrans now have a sun of their own, there should be no reason for hostility between our race and theirs. Perhaps we can start commercial trade with them. Imagine! Commerce over quintillions of miles of space!"

47

"And," interrupted Wade, "they can make the trip to this system in less time than it takes to get to Venus!"

"Meanwhile," said Morey, "let's get on with our own exploration."

They strapped themselves into the control seats once more and Arcot threw in the molecular drive to take them away from the sun toward which they had been falling.

When the great, hot disc of Sirius had once more diminished to a tiny white pinhead of light, Arcot turned the ship until old Sol once more showed plainly on the crosshairs of the aiming telescope in the rear of the vessel.

"Hold on," Arcot cautioned, "here we go again!"

Again he threw the little red tumbler that threw a flood of energy into the coils. The space about them seemed to shiver and grow dim.

Arcot had thrown more power into the coils this time, so the stars ahead of them instead of appearing violet were almost invisible; they were radiating in the ultra-violet now. And the stars behind them, instead of appearing to be green, had subsided to a dull red glow.

Arcot watched the dull red spark of Sirius become increasingly dimmer. Then, quite suddenly, a pale violet disc in front of them ballooned out of nowhere and slid off to one side.

The spaceship reeled, perking the men around in the control seats. Heavy safety relays thudded dully; the instruments flickered under a suddenly rising surge of power—then they were calm again. Arcot had snapped over the power switch.

"That," he said quietly, "is not so good."

"Threw the gyroscopes, didn't it?" asked Morey, his voice equally as quiet.

"It did—and I have no idea how far. We're off course and we don't know which direction we're headed."

VI

"WHAT'S THE MATTER?" asked Fuller anxiously.

Arcot pointed out the window at a red star that blazed in the distance. "We got too near the field of gravity of that young giant and he threw us for a loss. We drained out three-fourths of the energy from our coils and lost our bearings in the bargain. The attraction turned the gyroscopes and threw the ship out of line, so we no longer know where the sun is.

"Well, come on, Morey; all we can do is start a search. At this distance, we'd best go by Sirius; it's brighter and nearer." He looked at the instrument panel. "I was using the next lowest power and I still couldn't avoid that monster. This ship is just a little *too* hot to handle."

Their position was anything but pleasant. They must pick out from the vast star field behind them the one star that was home, not knowing exactly where it was. But they had one tremendous help—the photographs of the star field around Sol that they had taken at the last stop. All they had to do was search for an area that matched their photographs.

They found the sun at last, after they had spotted Sirius, but they had had to rotate the ship through nearly twenty-five degrees to do it. After establishing their bearings, they took new photographs for their files.

Meanwhile, Wade had been recharging the coils. When he was finished, he reported the fact to Arcot.

"Fine," Arcot said. "And from now on, I'm going to use the least possible amount of power. It certainly isn't safe to use more."

They started for the control room, much relieved. Arcot dived first, with Wade directly behind him. Wade decided suddenly to go into his room and stopped himself by grabbing a handhold. Morey, following close behind, bumped into him and was brought to rest, while Wade was pushed into his room.

But Fuller, coming last, slammed into Morey, who moved forward with new velocity toward the control room, leaving Fuller hanging at rest in the middle of the corridor.

"Hey, Morey!" he laughed. "Send me a skyhook! I'm caught!" Isolated as he was in the middle of the corridor, he couldn't push on anything and remained stranded.

"Go to sleep!" advised Morey. "It's the most comfortable bed you'll find!"

Wade looked out of his room just then. "Well, if it isn't old Weakmuscles Fuller! Weighs absolutely nothing and is still so weak he can't push himself around."

"Come on, though, Morey—give me a hand—I got you off dead center." Fuller flailed his hand helplessly.

"Use your brains, if you have any," said Morey, "and see what you can do. Come on, Wade—we're going."

Since they were going to use the space control, they would remain in free fall, and Fuller would remain helplessly suspended in mid-air.

The air of the ship suddenly seemed supercharged with energy as the space around them became gray; then the stars were all before them. The ship was moving forward again.

"Well, old pals," said Fuller, "at least I have traffic blocked fairly well if I feel like it, so eventually you'd have to help me. However—" He floundered clumsily as he removed one of his foam-rubber space-boots. "—my brains tell me that action is equal and opposite to reaction!" And he threw the boot with all possible velocity toward Morey!

The reaction of the motion brought him slowly but surely to a handhold in the wall.

In the meantime, the flying boot caught Morey in the chest with a pronounced *smack!* as he struggled vainly to

50

avoid it. Handicapped by the lack of friction, his arms were not quite powerful enough to move his mass as quickly as his legs might have done, for his inertia was as great as ever, so he didn't succeed in ducking.

"Round one!" called Arcot, laughing. "Won by Kid Fuller on a TKO! It appears he has brains and knows how to use them!"

"You win," laughed Morey. "I concede the battle!"

Arcot had cut off the space-strain drive by the time Fuller reached the control room, and the men set about making more observations. They took additional photographs and turned on the drive again.

Time passed monotonously after they had examined a few stars. There was little difference; each was but a scene of flaming matter. There was little interest in this work, and, as Fuller remarked, this was supposed to be a trip of exploration, not observation. They weren't astronomers; they were on a vacation. Why all the hard work? They couldn't do as good a job as an experienced astronomer, so they decided to limit their observations to those necessary to retrace their path to Earth.

"But we want to investigate for planets to land on, don't we?" asked Morey.

"Sure," agreed Fuller. "But do we have to hunt at random for them? Can't we look for stars like our own sun? Won't they be more apt to have planets like Sol's?"

"It's an idea," replied Morey.

"Well, why not try it then?" Fuller continued logically. "Let's pick out a G-O type sun and head for it."

They were now well out toward the edge of the Galaxy, some thirty thousand light years from home. Since they had originally headed out along the narrow diameter of the lens-shaped mass of stars that forms our Island Universe, they would reach the edge soon.

"We won't have much chance of finding a G-O this far out," Arcot pointed out. "We're about out of stars. We've left most of the Galaxy behind us."

"Then let's go on to another of the galactic nebulae,"

said Morey, looking out into the almost unbroken night of intergalactic space. Only here and there could they see a star, separated from its nearest neighbor by thousands of light years of empty space.

"You know," said Wade slowly, "I've been wondering about the progress along scientific lines that a race out here might make. I mean, suppose that one of those lonely stars had planets, and suppose intelligent life evolved on one of those planets. I think their progress would be much slower."

"I see what you mean," Arcot said. "To us, of Earth, the stars are gigantic furnaces a few light years away. They're titanic tests tubes of nature, with automatic reading devices attached, hung in the sky for us to watch. We have learned more about space from the stars than all the experiments of the physicists of Earth ever secured for us. It was in the atoms of the suns that we first counted the rate of revolutions of the electrons about their nuclei."

"Couldn't they have watched their own sun?" Fuller asked.

"Sure, but what could they compare it with? They couldn't see a white dwarf from here. They couldn't measure the paralax to the nearest star, so they would have no idea of stellar distances. They wouldn't know how bright S Doradus was. Or how dim Van Maanen's star was."

"Then," Fuller said speculatively, "they'd have to wait until one of their scientists invented the telectroscope."

Arcot shook his head. "Without a knowledge of nuclear physics, the invention of the telectroscope is impossible. The lack of opportunity to watch the stars that might teach them something would delay their knowledge of atomic structure. They might learn a great deal about chemistry and Newtonian physics, and go quite a ways with math, but even there they would be handicapped. Morey, for instance, would never have developed the autointegral calculus, to say nothing of tensor and spinor calculus, which were developed two hundred years ago, without the knowledge of the problems of space to develop the need. I'm afraid such a race would be quite a bit behind us in science.

"Suppose, on the other hand, we visit a race that's far

ahead of us. We'd better not stay there long; think what they might do to us. They might decide our ship was too threatening and simply wipe us out. Or they might even be so far advanced that we would mean nothing to them at all—like ants or little squalling babies." Arcot laughed at the thought.

"That isn't a very complimentary picture," objected Fuller. "With the wonderful advances we've made, there just isn't that much left to be able to say we're so little."

"Fuller, I'm surprised at you!" Arcot said. "Today, we are only opening our eyes on the world of science. Our race has only a few thousand years behind it and hundreds of millions yet to come. How can any man of today, with his freshly-opened eyes of science, take in the mighty pyramid of knowledge that will be built up in those long, long years of the future? It's too gigantic to grasp; we can't imagine the things that the ever-expanding mind of man will discover."

Arcot's voice slowed, and a far-off look came in his eyes.

"You might say there can be no greater energy than that of matter annihilation. I doubt that. I have seen hints of something new—an energy so vast—so transcendently tremendous—that it frightens me. The energies of all the mighty suns of all the galaxies—of the whole cosmos—in the hand of man! The energy of a billion billion billion suns! And every sun pouring out its energy at the rate of quintillions of horsepower every instant!

"But it's too great for man to have—I am going to forget it, lest man be destroyed by his own might."

Arcot's halting speech told of his intense thought—of a dream of such awful energies as man had never before conceived. His eyes looked unseeing at the black velvet of space with its few, scattered stars.

"But we're here to decide which way to go," he added with a sudden briskness as he straightened his shoulders. "Every now and then, I get a new idea and I—I sort of dream. That's when I'm most likely to see the solution. I think I know the solution now, but unless the need arises, I'm never going to use it. It's too dangerous a toy."

There was silence for a moment, then Morey said, quietly:

"I've got a course plotted for us. We'll leave this Galaxy at a steep angle—about forty-five degrees from the Galactic plane—to give us a good view of our own Galaxy. And we can head for one of the nebulae in that general area. What do you say?"

"I say," remarked Fuller, "that some of the great void without seems to have leaked into my own poor self. It's been thirty thousand years since I am going to have a meal this morning—whatever it is I mean—and I want another." He looked meaningfully at Wade, the official cook of the expedition.

Arcot suddenly burst out laughing. "So that's what I've been wanting!" It had been ten chronometer hours since they had eaten, but since they had been outracing light, they were now thirty thousand years in Earth's past.

The weightlessness of free fall makes it difficult to recognize normally familiar sensations, and the feeling of hunger is one of them. There was little enough work to be done, so there was no great need for nourishment, but the ordinary sensation of hunger is not caused by lack of nourishment, but an empty stomach.

Sleep was another problem. A restless body will not permit a tired brain to sleep, and though they had done a great deal of hard mental work, the lack of physical fatigue made sleep difficult. The usual "day" in space was forty hours, with thirty-hour waking periods and ten hours of sleep.

"Let's eat, then," Arcot decided. "Afterwards, we'll take a few photographs and then throw this ship into high and really make time."

Two hours later, they were again seated at the control board. Arcot reached out and threw the red switch. "I'm going to give her half power for ten seconds." The air about them seemed suddenly snapping with unprecedented power—then it was gone as the coil became fully charged.

"Lucky we shielded those relays," Arcot muttered. The tremendous surge of current set up a magnetic field that turned knives and forks and, as Wade found to his intense disgust, stopped watches that were not magnetically shielded.

Space was utterly black about them now; there wasn't the slightest hint of light. The ten seconds that Arcot had allowed dragged slowly. Then at last came the heavy crashing of the huge relays; the current flowed back into the storage coils, and space became normal again. They were alone in the blackness.

Morey dove swiftly for the observatory. Before them, there was little to see; the dim glow of nebulae millions of light years away was scarcely visible to the naked eye, despite the clarity of space.

Behind them, like a shining horizon, they saw the mass of the Galaxy for the first time as free observers.

Morey began to make swift calculations of the distance they had come by measuring the apparent change in diameter of the Galaxy.

Arcot floated into the room after him and watched as Morey made his observations and began to work swiftly with pencil and paper. "What do you make?" Arcot asked.

"Mmmmm. Let's see." Morey worked a moment with his slide rule. "We made good time! Twenty-nine light years in ten seconds! You had it on at half power—the velocity goes up as the cube of the power—doubling the power, then, gives us eight times the velocity—Hmmmmmmm." He readjusted the slide rule and slid the hairline over a bit. "We can make ten million light years in a little less than five days at full power.

"But I suggest we make another stop in six hours. That will put us about five radii, or half a million light years from the Galaxy. We'll need to take some more photographs to help us retrace our steps to Earth."

"All right, Morey," Arcot agreed. "It's up to you. Get

your photos here and we'll go on. By the way, I think you ought to watch the instruments in the power room; this will be our first test at full power. We figured we'd make twenty light years per second, and it looks as if it's going to be closer to twenty-four."

A few minutes later, Arcot seated himself at the control board and flipped on the intercom to the power room. "All ready, Morey? I just happened to think—it might be a good idea to pick out our galaxy now and start toward it."

"Let's wait," cautioned Morey. "We can't make a very careful choice at this distance, anyway; we're beyond the enlarging power range of the telectroscope here. In another half million light years, we'll have a much better view, and that comparatively short distance won't take us much out of our way."

"Wait a minute," said Fuller. "You say we're beyond the magnification range of the telectroscope. Then why would half a million light years out of ten million make that much difference?"

"Because of the limit of amplification in the tubes," Arcot replied. "You can only have so many stages of amplification; after that, you're amplifying noise. The whole principle of the vacuum tube depends on electronic emission; if you get *too much* amplification, you can hear every single electron striking the plate of the first tube by the time the thing reaches the last amplifying stage! In other words, if your incoming signal is weaker than the minimum noise level on the first amplifying stage, no amount of amplification will give you anything but more noise.

"The same is true of the telectroscope image. At this distance, the light signal from those galaxies is weaker than the noise level. We'd only get a flickering, blurred image. But if we go on another half million light years, the light signal from the nearer nebulae will be *stronger* than the base noise level, and full amplification will give us a good image on the screen."

Fuller nodded. "Okay, then let's go that additional half

million light years. I want to take a look at another galaxy."

"Right." Arcot turned to the intercom. "Ready, Morey?"

"Anytime you are."

"Here goes!" said Arcot. He pushed over the little red control.

At full power, the air filled with the strain of flowing energy and actually broke down in spots with the terrific electrical energy of the charge. There were little snapping sparks in the air, which, though harmless electrically, were hot enough to give slight burns, as Wade found to his sorrow.

"Yike! Say, why didn't you tell us to bring lightning rods?" he asked indignantly as a small spark snapped its way over his hand.

"Sorry," grinned Arcot, "but most people know enough to stay out of the way of those things. Seriously, though, I didn't think the electrostatic curvature would be so slow to adjust. You see, when we build up our light-rate distortion field, other curvatures are affected. We get some gravity, some magnetic, and some electrostatic field distortion, too. You can see what happens when they don't leak their energy back into the coil.

"But we're busy with the instruments; leave the motorman alone!"

Morey was calling loudly for tests. Although the ship seemed to be behaving perfectly, he wanted check tests to make sure the relays were not being burned, which would keep them from responding properly. By rerouting the current around each relay, Arcot checked them one by one.

It was just as they had finished testing the last one that Fuller yelled.

"Hey! *Look!*" He pointed out the broad viewport in the side of the ship.

Far off to their left and far to their right, they saw two shining ships paralleling their course. They were shining, sleek ships, their long, longitudinal windows glowing with white light. They seemed to be moving at exactly the same speed, holding grimly to the course of the *Ancient Mariner*. They bracketed the ship like an official guard, despite the terrific velocity of the Earthmen's ship.

Arcot stared in amazement, his face suddenly clouded in wonder. Morey, who had come up from the power room, stared in equal wonder.

Quickly, Wade and Fuller slid into the ray control seats. Their long practice with the rays had made them dead shots, and they had been chosen long before as the ship's official ray operators.

"Lord," muttered Morey as he looked at the ships, "where can they have come from?"

VII

SILENTLY, THE FOUR MEN watched the two ships, waiting for any hostile movement. There was a long, tense moment, then something happened for which three of them were totally unprepared.

Arcot burst into sudden laughter.

"Don't—ho—hoh-ho—oh—don't shoot!" he cried, laughing so hard it was almost impossible to understand him. "Ohoh—space—curved!" he managed to gasp.

For a moment more, Morey looked puzzled—then he was laughing as hard as Arcot. Helplessly, Wade and Fuller looked at them, then at each other. Then, suddenly, Wade caught the meaning of Arcot's remark and joined the other two in laughter.

"All right," said Fuller, still mystified, "when you half-witted physicists recover, please let me in on the joke!" He knew it had something to do with the mysterious ships, so he looked closely at them in hopes that he would get the point, too. When he saw it, he blinked in amazement. "Hey! What is this? Those ships are exact duplicates of the *Ancient Mariner!*"

"That—that's what I was laughing at," Arcot explained, wiping his eyes. "Four big, brave explorers, scared of their own shadows!"

"The light from our own ship has come back to us, due to the intense curvature of the space which encloses us. In normal space, a light ray would take hundreds of millions of years to travel all the way around the Universe and return to its point of origin. Theoretically, it would be possible to photograph our own Galaxy as it was thousands of millenia ago by the light which left it then and has traveled all the way around the curvature of space.

"But our space has such terrific curvature that it only takes a fraction of a second for light to make the trip. It has gone all the way around our little cosmos and come back again.

"If we'd shot at it, we would have really done ourselves in! The ray beam would go around and hit us from behind!"

"Say, that is a nice proposition!" laughed Fuller. "Then we'll be accompanied by those ghosts all the way? There goes the spirit 'nine fathoms deep' which moves the ship— the ghosts that work the sails. This will be a real *Ancient Mariner* trip!"

It was like that famed voyage in another way, too. The men found little to do as they passed on at high speed through the vast realm of space. The chronometer pointed out the hours with exasperating slowness. The six hours that were to elapse before the first stop seemed as many days. They had thought of this trip as a wonderful adventure in itself, but the soundless continued monotony was depressing. They wandered around, aimlessly. Wade tried to sleep, but after lying strapped in his bunk for half an hour, he gave up in despair.

Arcot saw that the strain of doing nothing was not going to be good for his little crew and decided to see what could be done about it.

He went down to the laboratory and looked for inspiration. He found it.

"Hey! Morey! Wade! Fuller! Come on down here! I've got an idea!" he called.

They came to find him looking meditatively at the power pack from one of the flying suits he had designed. He had taken the lux metal case off and was looking at the neat apparatus that lay within.

"These are equipped for use with the space suits, of course," Morey pointed out, "and that gives us protection against gases. But I wonder if we might install protection against mechanical injury—with intent to damage aforethought! In other words, why not equip these suits with a small invisibility apparatus? We have it on the ship, but we might need personal protection, too."

"Great idea," said Wade, "provided you can find room in that case."

"I think we can. We won't need to add anything but a few tuning devices, really, and they don't take a whale of a lot of power."

Arcot pointed out the places where they could be put; also, he replaced some of the old induction coils with one of his new storage cells and got far higher efficiency from the tubes.

But principally, it was something to do.

Indeed, it was so thoroughly something to do that the six hours had almost elapsed before they realized it. In a very short time, they returned again to the control room and strapped themselves in.

Arcot reached toward the little red switch that controlled the titanic energies of the huge coil below and pulled it back a quarter of the way.

"There go the ghosts!" he said. The images had quickly disappeared, seemingly leaping away from them at terrific speed as the space in which the ship was enclosed opened out more and more and the curvature decreased. They were further away from themselves!

Easing back a quarter at a time, to prevent sparks again flying about in the atmosphere of the ship, Arcot cut the power to zero, and the ship was standing still once more.

They hurriedly dived to the observatory and looked eagerly out the window.

Far, far behind them, floating in the marvelous, soft, utter blackness of space, was a shining disc made up of myriads of glowing points. And it didn't seem to be a huge thing at a great distance, but simply a small glowing object a few feet outside the window.

So perfectly clear was their view through the lux metal wall and the black, empty space that all sense of distance was lost. It seemed more a miniature model of their universe—a tiny thing that floated close behind them, unwavering, shining with a faint light, a heatless illumination that made everything in the darkened observatory glow very faintly. It was the light of three hundred million suns seen at a distance of three million million million miles! And it seemed small because there was nothing with which to compare it.

It was an amazingly beautiful thing, that tiny floating disc of light.

Morey floated over to the cameras and began to take pictures.

"I'd like to take a color shot of that," he said a few minutes later, "but that would require a direct shot through the reflector telescope and a time exposure. And I can't do that; the ship is moving."

"Not enough to make any difference," Arcot contradicted. "We're moving away from it in a straight line, and that thing is three quintillion miles away. We're not moving fast enough to cause any measurable contraction in a time exposure. As for having a steady platform, this ship weighs a quarter of a million tons and is held by gyroscopes. We won't shake it."

While Morey took the time exposure, Arcot looked at

the enlarged image in the telectroscope and tried to make angular measurements from the individual stars. This he found impossible. Although he could spot Betelgeuse and Antares because of their tremendous radiation, they were too close together for measurements; the angle subtended was too small.

Finally, he decided to use the distance between Antares and S Doradus in the Lesser Magellanic Cloud, one of the two clouds of stars which float as satellites to the Galaxy itself.

To double-check, he used the radius of the Galaxy as base to calculate the distance. The distances checked. The ship was five hundred thousand light years from home!

After all the necessary observations were made, they swung the ship on its axis and looked ahead for a landing place.

The nebulae ahead were still invisible to the naked eye except as points, but the telectroscope finally revealed one as decidedly nearer than the rest. It seemed to be a young Island Universe, for there was still a vast cloud of gas and dust from which stars were yet to be born in the central whorl—a single titanic gas cloud that stretched out through a million billion miles of space.

"Shall we head for that?" asked Arcot at last, as Morey finished his observations.

"I think it would be as good as any—there are more stars there than we can hope to visit."

"Well, then, here we go!"

Arcot dived for the control room, while Morey shut off the telectroscope and put the latest photographs in the file.

Suddenly space was snapping about him—they were off again. Another shock of surging energy—another—the ship leaped forward at tremendous speed—still greater—then they were rushing at top speed, and beside them ran the ghost ships of the *Ancient Mariner.*

Morey pushed himself into the control room just as Arcot, Wade, and Fuller were getting ready to start for the lab.

"We're off for quite a while, now," he said. "Our goal is about five days away. I suggest we stop at the end of four days, make more accurate measurements, then plan a closer stop.

"I think from now on we ought to sleep in relays, so that there will be three of us awake at all times. I'll turn in now for ten hours, and then someone else can sleep. Okay?"

It was agreed, and in the meantime the three on duty went down to the lab to work.

Arcot had finished the installation of the invisibility apparatus in his suit at the end of ten hours, much to his disappointment. He tested it, then cast about for something to do while Wade and Morey added the finishing touches to theirs.

Morey came down, and when Wade had finished his, which took another quarter of an hour, he took the off duty shift.

Arcot had gone to the library, and Morey was at work down below. Fuller had come up, looking for something to do, and had hit upon the excellent idea of fixing a meal.

He had just begun his preparations in the kitchen when suddenly the *Ancient Mariner* gave a violent leap, and the men, not expecting any weight, suddenly fell in different ways with terrific force!

Fuller fell half the length of the galley and was knocked out by the blow. Wade, asleep in bed, was awakened violently by the shock, and Morey, who had been strapped in his chair, was badly shaken.

Everyone cried out simultaneously—and Arcot was on his way to the control room. The first shock was but a forerunner of the storm. Suddenly the ship was hurled violently about; the air was shot through with great burning sparks; the snapping hiss of electricity was everywhere, and every pointed metal object was throwing streamers of blue electric flame into the air! The ship rocked, heaved, and cavorted wildly, as though caught in the play of titanic forces!

Scrambling wildly along the hand-holds, Arcot made his way towards the control room, which was now above, now below, and now to one side of him as the wildly variable acceleration shook the ship. Doggedly, he worked his way up, frequently getting severe burns from the flaming sparks.

Below, in the power room, the relays were crashing in and out wildly.

Then, suddenly, a new sound was added just as Arcot pulled himself into the control chair and strapped himself down. The radiation detector buzzed out its screaming warning!

"COSMIC RAYS!" Arcot yelled. "HIGH CONCENTRATION!"

He slapped at the switch which shot the heavy relux screens across every window in the ship.

There was a sudden crash and a fuse went out below— a fuse made of a silver bar two feet thick! In an instant, the flames of the burning sparks flared up and died. The ship cavorted madly, shaking mightily in the titanic, cosmic forces that surrounded it—the forces that made the highest energy form in the universe!

Arcot knew that nothing could be done with the power coil. It was drained; the circuit was broken. He shifted in the molecular drive, pushing the acceleration to four gravities, as high as the men could stand.

And still the powerful ship was being tossed about, the plaything of inconceivable forces. They lived only because the forces did not try to turn the ship more violently, not because of the strength of the ship, for nothing could resist the awful power around them.

As a guide, Arcot used the compass gyroscope, the only one not twisted far out of its original position; with it, he managed to steer a fairly straight course.

Meanwhile, in the power room, Wade and Morey were working frantically to get the space-strain drive coil recharged. Despite the strength-sapping strain of working under four gravities of acceleration, they managed to get the auxiliary power unit into operation. In a few moments, they had it pouring its energies into the coil-bank so that they could charge up the central drive coil.

Another silver bar fuse was inserted, and Wade checked the relays to make sure they were in working order.

Fuller, who had regained consciousness, worked his way laboriously down to the power room carrying three space-suits. He had stopped in the lab to get the power belts, and the three men quickly donned them to help them overcome the four-gravity pull.

Another half hour sped by as the bucking ship forced its way through the terrific field in space.

Suddenly they felt a terrific jolt again—then the ship was moving more smoothly, and gradually it was calm. They were through!

"Have we got power for the space-strain drive yet?" Arcot called through the intercom.

"Enough," Morey cried. "Try it!"

Arcot cut off the molecular motion drive, and threw in all the space-control power he had. The ship was suddenly supercharged with energy. It jarred suddenly—then was quiet. He allowed ten minutes to pass, then he cut off the drive and allowed the ship to go into free fall.

Morey's voice came over the intercom. "Arcot, things are really busted up down here! We had to haywire half the drive together."

"I'll be right down. Every instrument on the ship seems to be out of kilter!"

It was a good thing they had plenty of spare parts; some of the smaller relays had burned out completely, and several of the power leads had fused under the load that had been forced through them.

The space-strain drive had been leaking energy at a terrific rate; without further repair, it could not function much longer.

In the power room, Arcot surveyed the damage. "Well, boys, we'd better get to work. We're stranded here until we get that drive repaired!"

VIII

FORTY HOURS LATER, Arcot was running the ship smoothly at top speed once again. The four men had gone to bed after more than thirty hours of hard work. That, coupled with the exhaustion of working under four gravities, as they had while the ship was going through the storm, was enough to make them sleep soundly.

Arcot had awakened before the others and had turned on the drive after resetting their course.

After that was done, there was little to do, and time began to hang heavily on Arcot's hands. He decided to make a thorough inspection of the hull when the others awoke. The terrific strain might have opened cracks in the lux metal hull that would not be detectable from the inside because the inner wall was separated from the outer envelope.

Accordingly, he got out the spacesuits, making sure the oxygen tanks were full and all was ready. Then he went into the library, got out some books, and set about some calculations he had in mind.

When Morey woke, some hours later, he found Arcot still at work on his calculations.

"Hey!" he said, swinging himself into the chair beside Arcot, "I thought you'd be on the lookout for more cosmic rays!"

"Curious delusion, wasn't it?" asked Arcot blandly. "As a matter of fact, I've been busy doing some figuring. I think our chance of meeting another such region is about one in a million million million million. Considering those chances, I don't think we need to worry. I don't see how we ever met *one*—but the chances of hitting one are better than hitting two."

Just then Fuller stuck his head in the door.

"Oh," he said, "so you're at it already? Well, I wonder if one of you could tell me just what it was we hit? I've been so busy I haven't had a chance to think."

"Don't take the chance now, then," grinned Morey. "You might strain your brain."

"*Please!*" Fuller pleaded, wincing. "Not before breakfast. Just explain what that storm was."

"We simply came to a region in space where cosmic rays are created," explained Arcot.

Fuller frowned. "But there's nothing out here to generate cosmic rays!"

Arcot nodded. "True. I think I know their real source, but I believe I'll merely say they are created here. I want to do more work on this. My idea for an energy source greater than any other in the universe has been confirmed.

"At any rate, they are created in that space, a perfect vacuum, and the space there is distorted terrifically by the titanic forces at work. It is bent and twisted far out of the normal, even curvature, and it was that bumpy spot in space that threw us about so.

"When we first entered, using the space-strain drive, the space around the ship, distorted as it was, conflicted with the region of the cosmic ray generation and the ship lost out. The curvature of space that the ship caused was sometimes reinforced and sometimes cancelled out by the twisted space around it, and the tremendous surges of current back and forth from the main power coil to the storage coils caused the electric discharges that kept burning through the air. I notice we all got a few burns from that. The field was caused by the terrific surges of current, and that magnetic field caused the walls of the ship to heat up due to the generation of electric current in the walls."

Fuller looked around at the walls of the ship. "Well, the *Ancient Mariner* sure took a beating."

"As a matter of fact, I was worried about that," said Arcot. "Strong as that hull is, it might easily have been strained in that field of terrific force. If it happened to hit two 'space waves' at once, it might have given it an acceleration in two different directions at once, which would strain the walls with a force amounting to thousands of tons. I laid out the suits up front, and I think we might reasonably get out there and take a look at the old boat. When Wade gets up—well, well—speak of the devil! My, doesn't he look energetic?"

Wade's huge body was floating in through the library door. He was yawning sleepily and rubbing his eyes. It was evident he had not yet washed, and his growing beard, which was heavy and black on his cheeks, testified to his need for a shave. The others had shaved before coming into the library.

"Wade," said Arcot, "we're going outside, and we have to have someone in here to operate the airlock. Suppose you get to work on the hirsute adornment; there's an atomic hydrogen cutting torch down in the lab you can use, if you wish. The rest of us are going outside." Then Arcot's voice became serious. "By the way, don't try any little jokes like starting off with a little acceleration. I don't think you would —you've got good sense—but I like to make certain. If you did, we'd be left behind, and you'd never find us in the vast immensity of intergalactic space."

It wasn't a pleasant idea to contemplate. Each of the suits had a radio for communication with each other and with the ship, but they would only carry a few hundred miles. A mere step in space!

Wade shook his head, grinning. "I have no desire to be left all by myself on this ship, thank you. You don't need to worry."

A few minutes later, Arcot, Morey, and Fuller stepped out of the airlock and set to work, using power flashlights to examine the outer hull for any signs of possible strain.

The flashlights, equipped as they were with storage coils for power, were actually powerful searchlights, but in the airlessness of space, the rays were absolutely invisible. They could only be seen when they hit the relux inner wall at such an angle that they were reflected directly into the observer's eyes. The lux metal wall, being transparent, was naturally invisible, and the smooth relux, reflecting one hundred percent of the incident light, did not become illuminated, for illumination is the result of the scattering of light.

It was necessary to look closely and pass the beams over every square inch of the surface. However, a crack would be rough, and hence would scatter light and be even more readily visible than otherwise.

To their great relief, after an hour and a half of careful inspection, none of them had found any signs of a crack, and they went back into the ship to resume the voyage.

Again they hurled through space, the twin ghost ships following them closely. Hour after hour the ship went on. Now they had something else to do. They were at work calculating some problems that Arcot had suggested in connection with the velocities of motion that had been observed in the stars at the edge of the island universe they were approaching. Since these stars revolved about the mass of the entire galaxy, it was possible to calculate the mass of the entire universe by averaging the values from several stars. Their results were not exact, but they were reliable enough. They found the universe to have a mass of two hundred and fifty million suns, only a little less than the home Galaxy. It was an average-sized nebula.

Still the hours dragged as they came gradually nearer their goal—gradually, despite their speed of twenty-four light years per second!

At the end of the second day after their trouble with the cosmic ray field, they stopped for observation. They were now so near the Island Universe that the stars spread out in a huge disc ahead of them.

"About three hundred thousand light years distant, I should guess," said Morey.

"We know our velocity fairly accurately," said Wade. "Why can't we calculate the distance between two of these stars and then go on in?"

"Good idea," agreed Arcot. "Take the angle, will you, Morey? I'll swing the ship."

After taking their measurements, they advanced for one hour. Knowing this distance from experience, they were able to calculate the diameter of this galaxy. It turned out to be on the order of ninety thousand light years.

They were now much closer; they seemed, indeed, on the very edge of the giant universe. The thousands of stars flamed bright below them, stretching across their horizon more and more—a galaxy the eyes of men had never before seen at such close range! This galaxy had not yet condensed entirely to stars, and in its heart there still remained the vast gas cloud that would eventually be stars and planets. The vast misty cloud was plainly visible, glowing with a milky light like some vast frosted light bulb.

It was impossible to conceive the size of the thing; it looked only like some model, for they were still over a quarter of a million light years from it.

Morey looked up from his calculations. "I think we should be there in about three hours. Suppose we go at full speed for about two hours and then change to low speed?"

"You're the astronomical boss, Morey," said Arcot. "Let's go!"

They swung the ship about once more and started again. As they drew nearer to this new universe, they began to feel more interest in the trip. Things were beginning to happen!

The ship plunged ahead at full speed for two hours. They could see nothing at that velocity except the two ghost ships that were their ever-present companions. Then they stopped once more.

About them, they saw great suns shining. One was so close they could see it as a disc with the naked eye. But they could not see clearly; the entire sky was misty and the stars that were not close were blotted out. The room seemed to grow warm.

"Hey! Your calculations were off!" called Arcot. "We're getting out of here!"

Suddenly the air snapped and they were traveling at low speed under the drive of the space-strain apparatus. The entire space about them was lit with a dim violet glow. In ten minutes, the glow was gone and Arcot cut the drive.

They were out in ordinary dark space, with its star-studded blackness.

"What was the matter with my calculations?" Morey wanted to know.

"Oh, nothing much," Arcot said casually. "You were only about thirty thousand light years off. We landed right in the middle of the central gas cloud, and we were plowing through it at a relative velocity of around sixteen thousand miles per second! No wonder we got hot!

"We're lucky we didn't come near any stars in the process; if we had, we could have had to recharge the coil."

"It's a wonder we didn't burn up at that velocity," said Fuller.

"The gas wasn't dense enough," Arcot explained. "That gas is a better vacuum than the best pump could give you on Earth; there are fewer molecules per cubic inch than there are in a radio tube.

"But now that we're out of that, let's see if we can find a planet. No need to take photographs going in; if we want to find the star again, we can take photos as we leave. If we don't want to find it, we would just waste film.

"I'll leave it to Morey to find the star we want."

Morey set to work at once with the telescope, trying to find the nearest star of spectral type G-O, as had been agreed upon. He also wanted to find one of the same magnitude, or brilliance. At last, after investigating several such suns, he discovered one which seemed to fulfill all his wishes. The ship was turned, and they started toward the adventure they had really hoped to find.

As they rushed through space, the distorted stars shining vividly before them, they saw the one which was their

71

goal. A bright, slowly changing violet point on the cross-hairs of the aiming telescope.

"How far is it?" asked Arcot.

"About thirty light centuries," replied Morey, watching the star eagerly.

They drove on in silence. Then, suddenly, Morey cried out: "Look! It's gone!"

"What happened?" asked Arcot in surprise.

Morey rubbed his chin in thought. "The star suddenly flared brightly for an instant, then disappeared. Evidently, it was a G-O giant which had burned up most of the hydrogen that stars normally use for fuel. When that happens, a star begins to collapse, increasing in brilliance due to the heat generated by the gas falling toward the center of the star.

"Then other nuclear reactions begin to take place, and, due to the increased transparency of the star, a supernova is produced. The star blows away most of its gaseous envelope, leaving only the superdense core. In other words, it leaves a white dwarf." He paused and looked at Arcot. "I wonder if that star did have any planets?"

They all knew what he meant. What was the probable fate of beings whose sun had suddenly collapsed to a tiny, relatively cold point in the sky?

Suddenly, there loomed before them the dim bulk of the star, a disc already, and Arcot snapped the ship over to the molecular motion drive at once. He knew they must be close. Before them was the angry disc of the flaming white star.

Arcot swung the ship a bit to one side, running in close to the flaming star. It was not exceedingly hot, despite the high temperature and intense radiation, for the radiating surface was too small.

They swung about the star in a parabolic orbit, for, at their velocity, the sun could not hold them in a planetary orbit.

"Our velocity, relative to this star, is pretty high," Arcot announced. "I'm swinging in close so that I can use the star's attraction as a brake. At this distance, it will be about six gravities, and we can add to that a molecular drive braking of four gravities.

"Suppose you look around and see if there are any planets. We can break free and head for another star if there aren't."

Even at ten gravities of deceleration, it took several hours to reduce their speed to a point which would make it possible to head for any planet of the tiny sun.

Morey went to the observatory and swept the sky with the telectroscope.

It was difficult to find planets because the reflected light from the weak star was so dim, but he finally found one. He took angular readings on it and on the central sun. A little later, he took more readings. Because of the changing velocity of the ship, the readings were not too accurate, but his calculations showed it to be several hundred million miles out.

They were decelerating rapidly, and soon their momentum had been reduced to less than four miles a second. When they reached the planet, Arcot threw the ship into an orbit around it and began to spiral down.

Through the clear lux windows of the control room, the men looked down upon a bleak, frozen world.

IX

BELOW THE SHIP lay the unfamiliar panorama of an unknown world that circled, frozen, around a dim, unknown sun, far out in space. Cold and bleak, the low, rolling hills below were black, bare rock, coated in spots with a white sheen of what appeared to be snow, though each of the men realized it must be frozen air. Here and there ran

73

strange rivers of deep blue which poured into great lakes and seas of blue liquid. There were mighty mountains of deep blue crystal looming high, and in the hollows and cracks of these crystal mountains lay silent, motionless seas of deep blue, unruffled by any breeze in this airless world. It was a world that lay frozen under a dim, dead sun.

They continued over the broad sweep of the level, crystalline plain as the bleak rock disappeared behind them. This world was about ten thousand miles in diameter, and its surface gravity about a quarter greater than that of Earth.

On and on they swept, swinging over the planet at an altitude of less than a thousand feet, viewing the unutterably desolate scene of the cold, dead world.

Then, ahead of them loomed a bleak, dark mass of rock again. They had crossed the frozen ocean and were coming to land again—a land no more solid than the sea.

Everywhere lay the deep drifts of snow, and here and there, through valleys, ran the streams of bright blue.

"Look!" cried Morey in sudden surprise. Far ahead and to their left loomed a strange formation of jutting vertical columns, covered with the white burden of snow. Arcot turned a powerful searchlight on it, and it stood out brightly against the vast snowfield. It was a dead, frozen city.

As they looked at it, Arcot turned the ship and headed for it without a word.

It was hard ro realize the enormity of the catastrophe that had brought a cold, bleak death to the population of this world—death to an intelligent race.

Arcot finally spoke. "I'll land the ship. I think it will be safe for us all to leave. Get out the suits and make sure all the tanks are charged and the heaters working. It will be colder here than in space. Out there, we were only cooled by radiation, but those streams are probably liquid nitrogen, oxygen, and argon, and there's a slight atmosphere of hydrogen, helium and neon cooled to about fifty degrees Absolute. We'll be cooled by conduction and convection."

As the others got the suits ready, he lowered the ship gently to the snowy ground. It sank into nearly ten feet of snow. He turned on the powerful searchlight, and swept it around the ship. Under the warm beams, the frozen gasses evaporated, and in a few moments he had cleared the area around the ship.

Morey and the others came back with their suits. Arcot donned his, and adjusted his weight to ten pounds with the molecular power unit.

A short time later, they stepped out of the airlock onto the ice field of the frozen world. High above them glowed the dim, blue-white disc of the tiny sun, looking like little more than a bright star.

Adjusting the controls on the suits, the four men lifted into the tenuous air and headed toward the city, moving easily about ten feet above the frozen wastes of the snow field.

"The thing I don't understand," Morey said as they shot toward the city, "is why this planet is here at all. The intense radiation from the sun when it went supernova should have vaporized it!"

Arcot pointed toward a tall, oddly-shaped antenna that rose from the highest building of the city. "There's your answer. That antenna is similar to those we found on the planets of the Black Star; it's a heat screen. They probably had such antennas all over the planet.

"Unfortunately, the screen's efficiency goes up as the fourth power of the temperature. It could keep out the terrific heat of a supernova, but couldn't keep in the heat of the planet after the supernova had died. The planet was too cool to make the screen work efficiently!"

At last they came to the outskirts of the dead city. The vertical walls of the buildings were free of snow, and they could see the blank, staring eyes of the windows, and within, the bleak, empty rooms. They swept on through the frozen streets until they came to one huge building in the center. The doors of bronze had been closed, and through the windows they could see that the room had been piled high with some sort of insulating material, evidently used as a last-ditch attempt to keep out the freezing cold.

75

"Shall we break in?" asked Arcot.

"We may as well," Morey's voice answered over the radio. "There may be some records we could take back to Earth and have deciphered. In a time like this, I imagine they would leave some records, hoping that some race *might* come and find them."

They worked with molecular ray pistols for fifteen minutes tearing a way through. It was slow work because they had to use the heat ray pistols to supply the necessary energy for the molecular motion.

When they finally broke through, they found they had entered on the second floor; the deep snow had buried the first. Before them stretched a long, richly decorated hall, painted with great colored murals.

The paintings displayed a people dressed in a suit of some soft, white cloth, with blond hair that reached to their shoulders. They were shorter and more heavily built than Earthmen, perhaps, but there was a grace to them that denied the greater gravity of their planet. The murals portrayed a world of warm sunlight, green plants, and tall trees waving in a breeze—a breeze of air that now lay frozen on the stone floors of their buildings.

Scene after scene they saw—then they came to a great hall. Here they saw hundreds of bodies; people wrapped in heavy cloth blankets. And over the floor of the room lay little crystals of green.

Wade looked at the little crystals for a long time, and then at the people who lay there, perfectly preserved by the utter cold. They seemed only sleeping—men, women, and children, sleeping under a blanket of soft snow that evaporated and disappeared as the energy of the lights fell on it.

There was one little group the men looked at before they left the room of death. There were three in it—a young man, a fair, blonde young woman who seemed scarcely more than a girl, and between them, a little child. They were sleeping, arms about each other, warm in the arms of Death, the kindly Reliever of Pain.

76

Arcot turned and rose, flying swiftly down the long corridor toward the door.

"That was not meant for us," he said. "Let's leave."

The others followed.

"But let's see what records they left," he went on. "It may be that they wanted us to know their tragic story. Let's see what sort of civilization they had."

"Their chemistry was good, at least," said Wade. "Did you notice those green crystals? A quick, painless poison gas to relieve them of the struggle against the cold."

They went down to the first floor level, where there was a single great court. There were no pillars, only a vast, smooth floor.

"They had good architecture," said Morey. "No pillars under all the vast load of that building."

"And the load is even greater under this gravity," remarked Arcot.

In the center of the room was a great, golden bronze globe resting on a platform of marble. It must have been new when this world froze, for there was no sign of corrosion or oxidation. The men flew over to it and stood beside it, looking at the great sphere, nearly fifteen feet in diameter.

"A globe of their world," said Fuller, looking at it with interest.

"Yes," agreed Arcot, "and it was set up after they were sure the cold would come, from the looks of it. Let's take a look at it." He flew up to the top of it and viewed it from above. The whole globe was a carefully chiseled relief map, showing seas, mountains, and continents.

"Arcot—come here a minute," called Morey. Arcot dropped down to where Morey was looking at the globe. On the edge of one of the continents was a small raised globe, and around the globe, a circle had been etched.

"I think this is meant to represent this globe," Morey said. "I'm almost certain it represents this very spot. Now look over here." He pointed to a spot which, according to the scale of the globe, was about five thousand miles away. Projecting from the surface of the bronze globe was a little silver tower.

"They want us to go there," continued Morey. "This was erected only shortly before the catastrophe; they must have put relics there that they want us to get. They must have guessed that eventually intelligent beings would cross space; I imagine they have other maps like this in every large city.

"I think it's our duty to visit that cairn."

"I quite agree," assented Arcot. "The chance of other men visiting this world is infinitely small."

"Then let's leave this City of the Dead!" said Wade.

It gave them a sense of depression greater than that inspired by the vast loneliness of space. One is never so lonely as when he is with the dead, and the men began to realize that the original *Ancient Mariner* had been more lonely with strange companions than they had been in the depths of ten million light years of space.

They went back to the ship, floating through the last remnants of this world's atmosphere, back through the chill of the frozen gases to the cheering, warm interior of the ship.

It was a contrast that made each of them appreciate more fully the gift that a hot, blazing sun really is. Perhaps that was what made Fuller ask: "If this happened to a star so much like our sun, why couldn't it happen to Sol?"

"Perhaps it may," said Morey softly. "But the eternal optimism of man keeps us saying: 'It can't happen here.' And besides—" He put a hand on the wall of the ship. "—we don't ever have to worry about anything like that now. Not with ships like this to take us to a new sun—a new planet."

Arcot lifted the ship and flew over the cold, frozen ground beneath them, following the route indicated on the great globe in the dead city. Mile after mile of frozen ice fields flew by as they shot over it at three miles per second.

Suddenly, the bleak bulk of a huge mountain loomed gigantic before them. Arcot reversed the power and brought the ship to a stop. With the powerful searchlight, he swept the area, looking for the tower he knew should be here. At last, he made it out, a pyramid rather than a tower, and coated over with ice. They soon thawed out the frozen gasses by playing the energy of three powerful searchlights upon them, and in a few minutes the glint of gold showed through the melting ice and show.

"It looks," said Wade, "as though they have an outer wall of gold over a strong wall of iron or steel to protect it from corrosion. Certainly gold doesn't have enough tensile strength to hold itself up under this gravity—not in such masses as that."

Arcot brought the ship down beside the tower and the men once more went out through the airlock into the cold of the almost airless world. They flew across to the pyramid and looked for some means of entrance. In several places, they noticed hieroglyphics carved in great, foot-high characters. They searched in vain for a door until they noticed that the pyramid was not perfect, but truncated, leaving a flat area on top. The only joint in the walls seemed to be there, but there was no handle or visible methods of opening the door.

Arcot turned his powerful light on the surface and searched carefully for some opening device. He found a bas-relief engraving of a hand pointing to a corner of the door. He looked more closely and found a small jewel-like lens set in the metal.

Suddenly the men felt a vibration! There was a heavy click, and the door panel began to drop slowly.

"Get on it!" Arcot cried. "We can always break our way out if we're trapped!"

The four men leaped on it and sank slowly with it. The massive walls of the tower were nearly five feet thick, and made of some tough, white metal.

"Pure iron!" diagnosed Wade. "Or perhaps a silicon-iron alloy. Not as strong as steel, but very resistant to corrosion."

When the elevator stopped, they found themselves in a great chamber that was obviously a museum of the lost race. All around the walls were arranged models, books, and diagrams.

"We can never hope to take all this in our ship!" said Arcot, looking at the great collection. "Look—there's an old winged airplane! And a steam engine—and that's an electric motor! And that thing looks like some kind of an electric battery."

"But we can't take all that stuff," objected Fuller.

"No," Morey agreed. "I think our best bet would be to take all the books we can—making sure we get the introductory ones, so we can read the language.

"See—over there—they have marked those shelves with a single vertical mark. The ones next to them have two vertical marks, and next ones three. I suggest we load up with those books and take them to the ship."

The rest agreed, and they began carrying armloads of books, flying out through the top of the pyramid to the ship and back for more.

Instead of flying back to the pyramid for the last load, Arcot announced that he was going to leave a note for anyone who might come here later. While the others went back for the last load, he worked at drawing the "note".

"Let's see your masterpiece," said Morey as the three men returned to the ship with the last of the books.

Arcot had used a piece of tough, heavy plastic which would resist any corrosion the cold, almost airless world might have to offer.

Near the top, he had drawn a representation of their ship, and beneath it a representation of the route they had taken from universe to universe. The galaxy they were in was represented by a cloud of gas, its main identifying feature. Underneath the dotted line of their route through space, he had printed "200,000,000,000, u".

Then followed a little table. The numeral "1" followed by a straight bar, then "2" followed by two bars, and so on up to ten. Ten was represented by ten bars and, in addition, an S-shaped sign. Twenty was next, followed by twenty bars and two S-shaped signs. Thus he had worked up to "100".

The system he used would make it clear to any reasoning creature that he had used a decimal system and that the zeroes meant ten times.

Next below, he had drawn the planetary system of the frozen world, and the distance from the planet they were on to the central sun he labeled "u". Thus, the finders could reason that they had come a distance of two hundred billion units, where a distance of three hundred million miles was taken as the unit; they had, then, come from another galaxy. Certainly any creature with enough intelligence to reach this frozen world would understand this!

"Since the year of this planet is approximately eight times our own," Arcot continued, "I am indicating that we came here approximately five hundred years after the catastrophe." He pointed at several of the other drawings.

They left the message in the tower, and Arcot closed the door, leaving the pyramid exactly as it had been before they had come.

"Say!" Morey commented, "how did you open and close that door, anyway?"

Arcot grinned. "Didn't you notice the jewel at the corner? It was the lens of a photoelectric cell. My flashlight opened the door. I didn't figure it out; it just worked accidentally."

Morey raised an eyebrow. "But if the darned thing is so simple, any creature, intelligent or not, might be able to get in and destroy the records!"

Arcot looked at him. "And where are your savages going to come from? There are none on this planet, and anyone intelligent enough to build a spaceship isn't going to destroy the contents of the tower."

"Oh." Morey looked a little sheepish.

They went into the airlock and took off their suits. Then they began packing the precious books in specimen cases that had been brought for the purpose of preserving such things.

When the last of them was carefully stowed, they returned to the control room. They looked silently out across this strange, dead world, thinking how much it must have been like Earth. It was dead now, and frozen forever. The low hills that stretched out beneath them were dimly lighted by the weak rays of a shrunken sun. Three hundred million miles away, it glowed so weakly that this world received only a little more heat than it might have received from a small coal fire a mile away.

So weakly it flared that in this thin atmosphere of hydrogen and helium, its little corona glowed about it plainly, and even the stars around it shone brilliantly. The men could see one constellation that grouped itself in the outlines of a dragon, with the sun of this system as its cold, baleful eye.

Gradually, Arcot lifted the ship, and, as they headed out into space, they could see the dim frozen plains fall behind. It was as if a load of oppressing loneliness parted from them as they flew out into the vast spaces of the eternal stars.

X

Arcot looked speculatively at the star field in the great broad window before him. "We'll want to find another G-O sun, naturally, but I don't think we ought to go directly from here. If we did, we'd have to do a lot of backtracking to get back to this dead star. I suggest we go back to the edge of this galaxy, taking pictures on the way out, so that any future investigators can come in directly. It'll only take a few hours."

"I think you're right," agreed Morey. "Besides, that will

give us a wider choice of stars to pick our next G-O from. Let's get going."

Arcot moved the red switch, and the ship shot away at half speed. They watched the green image of the white dwarf fade and then suddenly flare up and become bright again as they outraced the light that had left it five centuries before.

They stopped and took more photographs so that the path could be marked. They stopped every light century until they reached a point where the star was merely a dim point, almost lost in the myriad of stars around it.

Then out to the edge of the galaxy they went, out toward their own universe.

"Arcot," Morey called, "let's go out, say one million light years into space, at an angle to this galaxy, and see if we can get both galaxies on one plate. It will make navigation between them easier."

"Good idea. We can get out and back in one day—and this 'time' won't count back on Earth, anyway." Since they would travel in the space-strain all the time, it would not count as Earth time.

Arcot pushed the red control all the way forward, and the ship began to move at its top velocity of twenty-four light years per second. The hours dragged heavily, as they had when they were coming in, and Arcot remained alone on watch while the others went to their rooms for some sleep, strapping their weightless bodies securely in the bunks.

It was hours later when Morey awoke with a sudden premonition of trouble. He looked at the chronometer on the wall—he had slept twelve hours! They had gone beyond the million light year mark! It didn't matter, except it showed that something had happened to Arcot.

Something had. Arcot was sound asleep in the middle of the library—exactly in the middle, floating in the room ten feet from each wall.

Morey called out to him, and Arcot awoke with a guilty start. "A fine sentry you make," said Morey caustically. "Can't even keep awake when all you have to do is sit here and see that we don't run into anything. We've gone more than our million light years already, and we're still going strong. Come on—snap out of it!"

"I'm sorry—I apologize—I know I shouldn't have slept, but it was so perfectly quiet here except for your deep-toned, musical snores that I couldn't help it," grinned Arcot. "Get me down from here and we'll stop."

"Get you down, nothing!" Morey snapped. "You stay right there while I call the others and we decide what's to be done with a sleeping sentry."

Morey turned and left to wake the others.

He had awakened Wade and told him what had happened, and they were on their way to wake up Fuller, when suddenly the air of the ship crackled around them! The space was changing! They were coming out of hyperspace!

In amazement, Morey and Wade looked at each other. They knew that Arcot was still floating helplessly in the middle of the room, but—

"Hold on, you brainless apes! We're turning around!" came Arcot's voice, full of suppressed mirth.

Suddenly they were both plastered against the wall of the ship under four gravities of acceleration! Unable to walk, they could only crawl laboriously toward the control room, calling to Arcot to shut off the power.

When Morey had left him stranded in the library, Arcot had decided it was high time he got to the floor. Quickly, he looked around for a means of doing so. Near him, floating in the air, was the book he had been reading, but it was out of reach. He had taken off his boots when he started to read, so the Fuller rocket method was out. It seemed hopeless.

Then, suddenly, came the inspiration! Quickly, he slipped off his shirt and began waving it violently in the air. He developed a velocity of about two inches a second—not very fast, but fast enough. By the time he had put his shirt back on, he had reached the wall.

After that, it was easy to shoot himself over to the door,

out into the corridor and into the control room without being seen by Morey, who was in Wade's room.

Just as Wade and Morey reached the doorway to the control room, Arcot decided it was time to shut the power off. Both of the men, laboring under more than eight hundred pounds of weight, were suddenly weightless. All the strength of their powerful muscles were expended in hurling them against the far wall.

The complaints were loud, but they finally simmered down to an earnest demand to know how in the devil Arcot had managed to get off dead center.

"Why, that was easy," he said airly. "I just turned on a little power; I fell under the influence of the weight and then it was easy to get to the control room."

"Come on," Wade demanded. "The truth! How did you get here?"

"Why, I just pushed myself here."

"Yes; no doubt. But how did you get hold of anything to push?"

"I just took a handful of air and threw it away and reached the wall."

"Oh, of course—and how did you hold the air?"

"I just took some air and threw it away and reached the wall."

Which was all they could learn. Arcot was going to keep his system secret, it seemed.

"At any rate," Arcot continued, "I am back in the control room, where I belong, and you are not in the observatory where you belong. Now get out of my territory!"

Morey pushed himself back to the observatory, and after a few minutes, his voice came over the intercom. "Let's move on a bit more, Arcot. We still can't get both galaxies on the same plate. Let's go on for another hour and take our pictures from that point."

Fuller had awakened and come in in the meantime, and he wanted to know why they didn't take some pictures from this spot.

"No point in it," said Morey. "We have the ones we took coming in; what we want is a wide-angle shot."

Arcot threw on the space-strain drive once more, and they headed on at top speed.

They were all in the control room, watching the instruments and joking—principally the latter—when it happened. One instant they were moving smoothly, weightlessly along. The next instant, the ship rocked as though it had been struck violently! The air was a snapping inferno of shooting sparks, and there came the sharp crash of the suddenly volatilized silver bar that was their main power fuse. Simultaneously, they were hurled forward with terrific force; the straps that held them in place creaked with the sudden strain, and the men felt weak and faint.

Consciousness nearly left them; they had been burned in a dozen places by the leaping sparks.

Then it was over. Except that the ghost ships no longer followed them, the *Ancient Mariner* seemed unchanged. Around them, they could see the dim glowing of the galaxies.

"Brother! We came near something!" Arcot cried. "It may be a wandering star! Take a look around, quick!"

But the dark of space seemed utterly empty around them as they coasted weightless through space. Then Arcot snapped off the lights of the control room, and in a moment his eyes had become accustomed to the dim lights.

It was dead ahead of them. It was a dull red glow, so dim it was scarcely visible. Arcot realized it was a dead star.

"There it is, Morey!" he said. "A dead star, directly ahead of us! Good God, how close are we?"

They were falling straight toward the dim red bulk.

"How far are we from it?" Fuller asked.

"At least several million—" Morey began. Then he looked at the distance recorded on the meteor detector. "ARCOT! FOR HEAVEN'S SAKE DO SOMETHING! THAT THING IS ONLY A FEW HUNDRED MILES AWAY!"

"There's only one thing to do," Arcot said tightly. "We

can never hope to avoid that thing; we haven't got the power. I'm going to try for an orbit around it. We'll fall toward it and give the ship all the acceleration she'll take. There's no time to calculate—I'll just pile on the speed until we don't fall into it."

The others, strapped into the control chairs, prepared themselves for the acceleration to come.

If the *Ancient Mariner* had dropped toward the star from an infinite distance, Arcot could have applied enough power to put the ship in a hyperbolic orbit which would have carried them past the star. But they had come in on the space drive, and had gotten fairly close before the gravitational field had drained the power from the main coil, and it was not until the space field had broken that they had started to accelerate toward the star. Their velocity would not be great enough to form an escape orbit.

Even now, they would fall far short of enough velocity to get into an elliptical orbit unless they used the molecular drive.

Arcot headed toward one edge of the star, and poured power into the molecular drive. The ship shot forward under an additional five and a half gravities of acceleration. Their velocity had been five thousand miles per second when they entered hyperspace, and they were swiftly adding to their original velocity.

They did not, of course, feel the pull of the sun, since they were in free fall in its field; they could only feel the five and a half gravities of the molecular drive. Had they been able to experience the pull of the star, they would have been crushed by their own weight.

Their speed was mounting as they drew nearer to the star, and Arcot was forcing the ship on with all the additional power he could get. But he knew that the only hope they had was to get the ship in a closed ellipse around the star, and a closed ellipse meant that they would be forever bound to the star as a planet! Helpless, for not even the titanic power of the *Ancient Mariner* could enable them to escape!

As the dull red of the dead sun ballooned toward them, Arcot said: "I think we'll make an orbit, all right, but we're going to be awfully close to the surface of that thing!"

The others were quiet; they merely watched Arcot and the star as Arcot made swift movements with the controls, doing all he could to establish them in an orbit that would be fairly safe.

It seemed like an eternity—five and a half gravities of acceleration held the men in their chairs almost as well as the straps of the antiacceleration units that bound them. When a man weighs better than half a ton, he doesn't feel like moving much.

Fuller whispered to Morey out of the corner of his sagging mouth. "What on Earth—I mean, what in Space is that thing? We're within only a few hundred miles, you said, so it must be pretty small. How could it pull us around like this?"

"It's a dead white dwarf—a 'black dwarf', you might say," Morey replied. "As the density of such matter increases, the volume of the star depends less and less on its temperature. In a dwarf with the mass of the sun, the temperature effect is negligible; it's the action of the forces within the electron-nucleon gas which makes up the star that reigns supreme.

"It's been shown that if a white dwarf—or a black one—is increased in mass, it begins to decrease sharply in volume after a certain point is reached. In fact, no *cold* star can exist with a volume greater than about one and a half times the mass of the sun—as the mass increases and the pressure goes up, the star shrinks in volume because of the degenerate matter in it. At a little better than 1.4 times the mass of the sun—our sun, I mean: Old Sol—the star would theoretically collapse to a point.

"That has almost happened in this case. The actual limit is when the star has reached the density of a neutron, and this star hasn't collapsed that far by a long shot.

"But that star is only forty kilometers—*or less than twenty-five miles* in diameter!"

It took nearly two hours of careful juggling to get an orbit which Arcot considered reasonably circular.

And when they finally did, Wade looked at the sky above them and shouted: "Say, look! What are all those streaks?"

Arcing up from the surface of the dull red plain below them and going over the ship, were several dim streaks of light across the sky. One of them was brighter than the rest, a bright white streak. The streaks didn't move; they seemed to have been painted on the sky overhead, glowing bands of unwavering light.

"Those," said Arcot, "are the nebulae. That wide streak is the one we just left. The bright streak must be a nearby star.

"They look like streaks because we're moving so fast in so small an orbit." He pointed to the red star beneath them. "We're less than twenty miles from the center of that thing! We're almost exactly thirty kilometers from its center, or about ten kilometers from its surface! But, because of it's great mass, our orbital velocity is something terrific!

"We're going around that thing better than three hundred times every second; our 'year' is three milliseconds long! Our orbital velocity is *seven hundred thousand kilometers per second!*

"We're moving along at about a fifth of the speed of light!"

"Are we safe in this orbit?" Fuller asked.

"Safe enough," said Arcot bitterly. "So damned safe that I don't see how we'll ever break free. We can't pull away with all the power on this ship. We're trapped!

"Well, I'm worn out from working under all that gravity; let's eat and get some sleep."

"I don't feel like sleeping," said Fuller. "You may call this safe, but it would only take an instant to fall down to the surface of that thing there." He looked down at their inert, but titanically powerful enemy whose baleful glow seemed even now to be burning their funeral pyre.

"Well," said Arcot, "falling into it and flying off into space are two things you don't have to worry about. If we started toward it, we'd be falling, and our velocity would increase; as a result, we'd bounce right back out again. The magnitude of the force required to make us fall into that sun is appalling! The gravitational pull on us now amounts to about five *billion* tons, which is equalized by the centrifugal force of our orbital velocity. Any tendency to change it would be like trying to bend a spring with that much resistance.

"We'd require a tremendous force to make us either fall into that star—or get away from it.

"To escape, we have to lift this ship out against gravity. That means we'd have to lift about five million tons of mass. As we get farther out, our weight will decrease as the gravitational attraction drops off, but we would need such vast amounts of energy that they are beyond human conception.

"We have burned up two tons of matter recharging the coils, and are now using another two tons to recharge them again. We need at least four tons to spare, and we only started out with twenty. We simply haven't got fuel enough to break loose from this star's gravitational hold, vast as the energy of matter is. Let's eat, and then we can sleep on the problem."

Wade cooked a meal for them, and they ate in silence, trying to think of some way out of their dilemma. Then they tried to sleep on the problem, as Arcot had suggested, but it was difficult to relax. They were physically tired; they had gone through such great strains, even in the short time that they had been maneuvering, that they were very tired.

Under a pull five times greater than normal gravity, they had tired in one-fifth the time they would have at one gravity, but their brains were still wide awake, trying to think of some way—*any way*—to get away from the dark sun.

But at last sleep came.

ISLANDS OF SPACE

XI

MOREY THOUGHT he was the first to waken when, seven hours later, he dressed and dove lightly, noiselessly, out into the library. Suddenly, he noticed that the telectroscope was in operation—he heard the low hum of its smoothly working director motors.

He turned and headed back toward the observatory. Arcot was busy with the telectroscope.

"What's up, Arcot?" he demanded.

Arcot looked up at him and dusted off his hands. "I've just been gimmicking up the telectroscope. We're going around this dead dwarf once every three milliseconds, which makes it awfully hard to see the stars around us. So I put in a cutoff which will shut the telectroscope off most of the time; it only looks at the sky once every three milliseconds. As a result, we can get a picture of what's going on around us very easily. It won't be a steady picture, but since we're getting a still picture three hundred times a second, it will be better than any moving picture film ever projected as far as accuracy is concerned.

"I did it because I want to take a look at that bright streak in the sky. I think it'll be the means to our salvation—if there is any."

Morey nodded. "I see what you mean; if that's another white dwarf—which it most likely is—we can use it to escape. I think I see what you're driving at."

"If it doesn't work," Arcot said coolly, "we can profit by the example of the people we left back there. Suicide is preferable to dying of cold."

Morey nodded. "The question is: How helpless are we?"

"Depends entirely on that star; let's see if we can get a focus on it."

At the orbital velocity of the ship, focussing on the star was indeed a difficult thing to do. It took them well over an hour to get the image centered in the screen without its drifting off toward one edge; it took even longer to get the focus close enough to a sphere to give them a definite reading on the instruments. The image had started out as a streak, but by taking smaller and smaller sections of the streak at the proper times, they managed to get a good, solid image. But to get it bright enough was another problem; they were only picking up a fraction of the light, and it had to be amplified greatly to make a visible image.

When they finally got what they were looking for, Morey gazed steadily at the image. "Now the job is to figure the distance. And we haven't got much parallax to work with."

"If we compute in the timing in our blinker system at opposite sides of the orbit, I think we can do it," Arcot said.

They went to work on the problem. When Fuller and Wade showed up, they were given work to do—Morey gave them equations to solve without telling them to what the figures applied.

Finally Arcot said: "Their period about the common center of gravity is thirty-nine hours, as I figure it."

Morey nodded. "Check. And that gives us a distance of two million miles apart."

"Just what are you two up to?" asked Fuller. "What good is another star? The one we're interested in is this freak underneath us."

"No," Arcot corrected, "we're interested in getting *away* from the one beneath us, which is an entirely different matter. If we were midway between this star and that one, the gravitational effects of the two would be cancelled out, since we would be pulled as hard in one direction as the other. Then we'd be free of both pulls and could escape!

"If we could get into that neutral area long enough to turn on our space strain drive, we could get away between them fast. Of course, a lot of our energy would be **eaten** up, but we'd get away.

"That's our only hope," Arcot concluded.

"Yes, and what a whale of a hope it is," Wade snorted sarcastically. "How are you going to get out to a point halfway between these two stars when you don't have enough power to lift this ship a few miles?"

"If Mahomet can not go to the mountain," misquoted Arcot, "then the mountain must come to Mahomet."

"What are you going to do?" Wade asked in exasperation. "Beat Joshua? He made the sun stand still, but this is a job of throwing them around!"

"It is," agreed Arcot quietly, "and I intend to throw that star in such a way that we can escape between the twin fields! We can escape between the hammer and the anvil as millions of millions of millions of tons of matter crash into each other."

"And you intend to swing that?" asked Wade in awe as he thought of the spectacle there would be when two suns fell into each other. "Well, I don't want to be around."

"You haven't any choice," Arcot grinned. Then his face grew serious. "What I want to do is simple. We have the molecular ray. Those stars are hot. They don't fall into each other because they are rotating about each other. Suppose that rotation were stopped—stopped suddenly and completely? The molecular ray acts catalytically; we won't supply the power to stop that star, the star itself will. All we have to do is cause the molecules to move in a direction opposite to the rotation. We'll supply the impulse, and the star will supply the energy!

"Our job will be to break away when the stars get close enough; we are really going to hitch our wagon to a star!

"The mechanics of the job are simple. We will have to calculate when and how long to use the power, and when and how quickly to escape. We'll have to use the main power board to generate the ray and project it instead of the little ray units. With luck, we ought to be free of this star in three days!"

Work was started at once. They had a chance of life in sight, and they had every intention of taking advantage of it! The calculating machines they had brought would certainly prove worth their mass in this one use. The observations were extremely difficult because the ship was rocketing around the star in such a rapid orbit. The calculations of the mass and distance and orbital motion of the other star were therefore very difficult, but the final results looked good.

The other star and this one formed a binary, the two being of only slightly different mass and rotating about each other at a distance of roughly two million miles.

The next problem was to calculate the time of fall from that point, assuming that it would stop instantaneously, which would be approximately true.

The actual fall would take only seven hours under the tremendous acceleration of the two masses! Since the stars would fall toward each other, the ship would be drawn toward the falling mass, and since their orbit around the star took only a fraction of a second to complete, they had to make sure they were in the right position at the halfway point just before collision occurred. Also, their orbit would be greatly perturbed as the star approached, and it was necessary to calculate that in, too.

Arcot calculated that in twenty-two hours, forty-six minutes, they would be in the most favorable position to start the fall. They could have started sooner, but there were some changes that had to be made in the wiring of the ship before they could start using the molecular ray at full power.

"Well," said Wade as he finally finished the laborious computations, "I hope we don't make a mistake and get caught between the two! And what happens if we find we haven't stopped the star after all?"

"If we don't hit it exactly the first time," Morley replied, "we'll have to juggle the ray until we do."

They set to work at once, installing the heavy leads to the ray projectors, which were on the outside of the hull in countersunk recesses. Morey and Wade had to go outside the ship to help attach the cables.

ISLANDS OF SPACE

Out in space, floating about the ship, they were still weightless, for they, too, were supported by centrifugal force.

The work of readjusting the projectors for greater power was completed in an hour and a quarter, which still left over twenty hours before they could use them. During the next ten hours, they charged the great storage coils to capacity, leaving the circuits to them open, controlled by the relays only. That would keep the coils charged, ready to start.

Finally, Wade dusted off his hands and said: "We're all ready to go mechanically, and I think it would be wise if we were ready physically, too. I know we're not very tired, but if we sit around in suspense we'll be as nervous as cats when the time comes. I suggest we take a couple of sleeping tablets and turn in. If we use a mild shock to awaken us, we won't oversleep."

The others agreed to the plan and prepared for their wait.

Awakened two hours before the actual moment of action, Wade prepared breakfast, and Morey took observations. He knew just where the star should be according to their calculations, and looked for it there. He breathed a sigh of relief—it was exactly in place! Their mathematics they had been sure of, but on such a rapidly moving machine, it was exceedingly difficult to make good observations.

The two hours seemed to drag interminably, but at last Arcot signalled for the full power of the molecular rays. They waited, breathlessly, for some response. Nearly twenty seconds later, the other sun went out.

"We did it!" said Wade in a hushed voice. It was almost a shock to realize that this ship had power enough to extinguish a sun!

Arcot and Morey weren't awed; they didn't have time. There were other things to do and do fast.

They had checked the time required for them to see that the white dwarf had gone out. Half of this gave them the distance from the star in light seconds.

The screen had already been rigged to flash the information into a computer, which in turn gave a time signal to the robot pilot that would turn on the drive at precisely the right instant. There was no time for human error here; the velocities were too great and the time for error too small.

Then they waited. They had to wait for seven hours spinning dizzily around an improbably tiny star with an equally improbably titanic gravitational field. A star only a couple of dozens of miles across, and yet so dense that it weighed half a million times as much as the Earth! And they had to wait while another star like it, chilled now to absolute zero, fell toward them!

"I wish we could stay around to see the splash," Arcot said. "It's going to be something to see. All the kinetic energy of those two masses slamming into each other is going to be a blaze of light that will really be something!"

Wade was looking nervously at the telectroscope plate. "I wish we could see that other sun. I don't like the idea of a thing that big creeping up on us in the dark."

"Calm down," Morey said quietly. "It's out of our hands now; we took a chance, and it was a chance we *had* to take. If you want to watch something, watch Junior down there. It's going to start doing some pretty interesting tricks."

As the dense black sun approached them, Junior, as Morey had called it, did begin to do tricks. At first they seemed to be optical effects, as though the eye itself were playing tricks. The red, glowing ball beneath them began to grow transparent around its surface, leaving an opaque red core which seemed to be shrinking slowly.

"What's happening?" Fuller asked.

"Our orbit around the star is becoming more and more elliptical," Arcot replied. "As the other sun pulls us, the star beneath us grows smaller with the distance; then, as we begin to fall back toward it, it grows larger again. Since this is taking place many hundreds of times per second, the visual pictures all seem to blend in together."

"Watch the clock," Morey said suddenly, pointing.

The men watched tensely as the hand moved slowly around.

96

"Ten —nine —eight —seven —six —five —four —three —two —one —ZERO!"

A relay slammed home, and almost instantaneously, everyone on the ship was slammed into unconsciousness.

XII

Hours later, Arcot regained consciousness. It was quiet in the ship. He was still strapped in his seat in the control room. The relux screens were in place, and all was perfectly peaceful. He didn't know whether the ship was motionless or racing through space at a speed faster than light, and his first semiconscious impulse was to see.

He reached out with an arm that seemed to be made of dry dust, ready to crumble; an arm that would not behave. His nerves were jumping wildly. He pulled the switch he was seeking, and the relux screens dropped down as the motors pulled them back.

They were in hyperspace; beside them rode the twin ghost ships.

Arcot looked around, trying to decide what to do, but his brain was clogged. He felt tired; he wanted to sleep. Scarcely able to think, he dragged the others to their rooms and strapped them in their bunks. Then he strapped himself in and fell asleep almost at once.

Still more hours passed, then Arcot was waking slowly to insistent shaking by Morey.

"Hey! Arcot! Wake up! ARCOT! HEY!"

Arcot's ears sent the message to his brain, but his brain tried to ignore it. At last he slowly opened his eyes.

"Huh?" he said in a low, tired voice.

"Thank God! I didn't know whether you were alive or not. None of us remembered going to bed. We decided you must have carried us there, but you sure looked dead."

"Uhuh?" came Arcot's unenthusiastic rejoinder.

"Boy, is he sleepy!" said Wade as he drifted into the room. "Use a wet cloth and some cold water, Morey."

A brisk application of cold water brought Arcot more nearly awake. He immediately clamored for the wherewithal to fill an aching void that was making itself painfully felt in his midsection.

"He's all right!" laughed Wade. "His appetite is just as healthy as ever!"

They had already prepared a meal, and Arcot was promptly hustled to the galley. He strapped himself into the chair so that he could eat comfortably, and then looked around at the others. "Where the devil are we?"

"That," replied Morey seriously, "as just what we wanted to ask you. We haven't the beginnings of an idea. We slept for two days, all told, and by now we're so far from all the Island Universes that we can't tell one from another. We have no idea where we are.

"I've stopped the ship; we're just floating. I'm sure I don't know what happened, but I hoped you might have an idea."

"I have an idea," said Arcot. "I'm hungry! You wait until after I've eaten, and I'll talk." He fell to on the food.

After eating, he went to the control room and found that every gyroscope in the place had been thrown out of place by the attractions they had passed through. He looked around at the meters and coils.

It was obvious what had happened. Their attempt to escape had been successful; they had shot out between the stars, into the space. The energy had been drained from the power coil, as they had expected. Then the power plant had automatically cut in, recharging the coils in two hours. Then the drive had come on again, and the ship had flashed on into space. But with the gyroscopes as erratic as they were, there was no way of knowing which direction they had come; they were lost in space!

"Well, there are lots of galaxies we can go to," said Arcot. "We ought to be able to find a nice one and stay there if we can't get home again."

"Sure," Wade replied, "but I like Earth! If only we hadn't all passed out! What caused that, Arcot?"

Arcot shrugged. "I'm sure I don't know. My only theory is that the double gravitational field, plus our own power field, produced a sort of cross-product that effected our brains.

"At any rate, here we are."

"We certainly are," agreed Morey. "We can't possibly back track; what we have to do is identify our own universe. What identifying features does it have that will enable us to recognize it?

"Our Galaxy has two 'satellites', the Greater and Lesser Magellanic Clouds. If we spent ten years photographing and studying and comparing with the photographs we already have, we might find it. We know that system will locate the Galaxy, but we haven't the time. Any other suggestions?"

"We came out here to visit planets, didn't we?" asked Arcot. "Here's our chance—and our only chance—of getting home, as far as I can see. We can go to any galaxy in the neighborhood—within twenty or thirty million light years—and look for a planet with a high degree of civilization.

"Then we'll give them the photographs we have, and ask them if they've any knowledge of a galaxy with two such satellites. We just keep trying until we find a race which has learned through their research. I think that's the easiest, quickest, and most satisfactory method. What do you think?"

It was the obvious choice, and they all agreed. The next proposition was to select a galaxy.

"We can go to any one we wish," said Morey, "but we're now moving at thirty thousand miles per second; it would take us quite a while to slow down, stop, and go in the other direction. There's a nice, big galactic nebula right in front of us, about three days away—six million light years. Any objections to heading for that?"

The rest looked at the glowing point of the nebula. Out in space, a star is a hard, brilliant, dimensionless point of light. But a nebula glows with a faint mistiness; they are so far away that they never have any bright glow, such as stars have, but they are so vast, their dimensions so great, that even across millions of light years of space they appear as tiny glowing discs with faint, indistinct edges. As the men looked out of the clear lux metal windows, they saw the tiny blur of light on the soft black curtain of space.

It was as good a course as any, and the ship's own inertia recommended it; they had only to redirect the ship with greater accuracy.

Setting the damaged gyroscopes came first, however. There were a number of things about the ship that needed readjustment and replacement after the strain of escaping from the giant star.

After they had made a thorough inspection Arcot said:

"I think we'd best make all our repairs out here. That flame that hit us burned off our outside microphone and speaker, and probably did a lot of damage to the ray projectors. I'd rather not land on a planet unarmed; the chances are about fifty-fifty that we'd be greeted with open cannon muzzles instead of open arms."

The work inside was left to Arcot and Fuller, while Morey and Wade put on spacesuits and went out onto the hull.

They found surprisingly little damage—far less than they had expected. True, the loudspeaker, the microphone, and all other instruments made of ordinary matter had been burned off clean. They didn't even have to clean out the spaces where they had been recessed into the wall. At a temperature of ten thousand degrees, the metals had all boiled away—even tungsten boils at seven thousand degrees, and all other normal matter boils even more easily.

The ray projectors, which had been adjusted for the high power necessary to stop a sun in its orbit, were readjusted for normal power, and the heat beams were replaced.

After nearly four hours work, everything had been checked, from relays and switch points to the instruments and gyroscopes. Stock had been taken, and they found they were running low on replacement parts. If anything more happened, they would have to stop using some of the machinery and break it up for spare parts. Of their original supply of twenty tons of lead fuel, only ten tons of the metal were left, but lead was a common metal which they could easily pick up on any planet they might visit. They could also get a fresh supply of water and refill their air tanks there.

The ship was in as perfect condition as it had ever been, for every bearing had been put in condition and the generators and gyroscopes were running smoothly.

They threw the ship into full speed and headed for the galaxy ahead of them.

"We are going to look for intelligent beings," Arcot reminded the others, "so we'll have to communicate with them. I suggest we all practice the telepathic processes I showed you—we'll need them."

The time passed rapidly with something to do. They spent a considerable part of it reading the books on telepathy that Arcot had brought, and on practicing it with each other.

By the end of the second day of the trip, Morey and Fuller, who had peculiarly adaptable minds, were able to converse readily and rapidly, Fuller doing the projecting and Morey the receiving. Wade had divided his time about equally between projecting and reading, with the result that he could do neither well.

Early on the fourth day, they entered the universe toward which they were heading. They had stopped at about half a million light years and decided that a large local cluster of very brilliant suns promised the best results, since the stars were closer together there, and there were many of the yellow G-O type for which they were seeking.

They had penetrated into the galaxy as far as was safe, using half speed; then, at lower speeds, they worked toward the local cluster.

101

Arcot cut the drive several light years from the nearest sun. "Well, we're where we wanted to be; now what do we do? Morey, pick us out a G-O star. We await your royal command to move."

After a few minutes at the telectroscope, Morey pointed to one of the pinpoints of light that gleamed brightly in the sky. "That one looks like our best bet. "It's a G-O a little brighter than Sol."

Morey swung the ship about, pointing the axis of the ship in the same direction as its line of flight. The observatory had been leading, but now the ship was turned to its normal position.

They shot forward, using the space-strain drive, for a full hour at one-sixteenth power. Then Arcot cut the drive, and the disc of the sun was large before them.

"We're going to have a job cutting down our velocity; we're traveling pretty fast, relative to that sun," Arcot told the others. Their velocity was so great that the sun didn't seem to swerve them greatly as they rushed nearer. Arcot began to use the molecular drive to brake the ship.

Morey was busy with the telectroscope, although greatly hampered by the fact that it was a feat of strength to hold his arm out at right angles to his body for ten seconds under the heavy acceleration Arcot was applying.

"This method works!" called Morey suddenly. "The Fuller System For Finding Planets has picked another winner! Circle the sun so that I can get a better look!"

Arcot was already trying vainly to decrease their velocity to a figure that would permit the attraction of the sun to hold them in its grip and allow them to land on a planet.

"As I figure it," Arcot said, "we'll need plenty of time to come to rest. What do you think, Morey?"

Morey punched figures into the calculator. "Wow! Somewhere in the neighborhood of a hundred days, using all the acceleration that will be safe! At five gravities, reducing our present velocity of twenty-five thousand miles per second to zero will take approximately twenty-four hundred hours—

one hundred days! We'll have to use the gravitational attraction of that sun to help us."

"We'll have to use the space control," said Arcot. "If we move close to the sun by the space control, all the energy of the fall will be used in overcoming the space-strain coil's field, and thus prevent our falling. When we start to move away again, we will be climbing against that gravity, which will aid us in stopping. But even so, it will take us about three days to stop. We wouldn't get anywhere using molecular power; that giant sun was just too damned generous with his energy of fall!"

They started the cycles, and, as Arcot had predicted, they took a full three days of constant slowing to accomplish their purpose, burning up nearly three tons of matter in doing so. They were constantly oppressed by a load of five gravities except for the short intervals when they stopped to eat and when they were moving in the space control field. Even in sleeping, they were forced to stand the load.

The massive sun was their principal and most effective brake. At no time did they go more than a few dozen million miles from the primary, for the more intense the gravity, the better effect they got.

Morey divided his time between piloting the ship while Arcot rested, and observing the system. By the end of the third day, he had made very creditable progress with his map.

He had located only six planets, but he was certain there were others. For the sake of simplicity, he had assumed circular orbits and calculated their approximate orbital velocities from their distance from the sun. He had determined the mass of the sun from direct weighings aboard their ship. He soon had a fair diagram of the system constructed mathematically, and experimental observation showed it to be a very close approximation.

The planets were rather more massive than those of Sol. The innermost planet had a third again the diameter of Mercury and was four million miles farther from the primary. He named it Hermes. The next one, which he named Aphrodite, the Greek goddess corresponding to the Roman Venus, was only a little larger than Venus and was some eight million miles farther from its primary—seventy-five million miles from the central sun.

The next, which Morey called Terra, was very much like Earth. At a distance of a hundred and twenty-four million miles from the sun, it must have received almost the same amount of heat that Earth does, for this sun was considerably brighter than Sol.

Terra was eight thousand two hundred miles in diameter, with a fairly clear atmosphere and a varying albedo which indicated clouds in the atmosphere. Morey had every reason to believe that it might be inhabited, but he had no proof because his photographs were consistently poor due to the glare of the sun.

The rest of the planets proved to be of little interest. In the place where, according to Bode's Law, another planet, corresponding to Mars, should have been, there was only a belt of asteroids. Beyond this was still another belt. And on the other side of the double asteroid belt was the fourth planet, a fifty-thousand-mile-in-diameter methane-ammonia giant which Morey named Zeus in honor of Jupiter.

He had picked up a couple of others on his plates, but he had not been able to tell anything about them as yet. In any case, the planets Aphrodite and Terra were by far the most interesting.

"I think we picked the right angle to come into this system," said Arcot, looking at Morey's photographs of the wide bands of asteroids. They had come into the planetary group at right angles to the plane of the ecliptic, which had allowed them to miss both asteroid belts.

They started moving toward the planet Terra, reaching their objective in less than three hours.

The globe beneath them was lit brightly, for they had approached it from the daylight side. Below them, they could see wide, green plains and gently rolling mountains, and in a great cleft in one of the mountain ranges was a shimmering lake of clearest blue.

The air of the planet screamed about them as they dropped down, and the roar in the loudspeaker grew to a mighty cataract of sound. Morey turned down the volume.

The sparkling little lake passed beneath them as they shot on, seventy-five miles above the surface of the planet. When they had first entered the atmosphere, they had the impression of looking down on a vast, inverted bowl whose edge rested on a vast, smooth table of deep violet velvet. But as they dropped and the violet became bluer and bluer, they experienced the strange optical illusion of "flopping" of the scene. The bowl seemed to turn itself inside out, and they were looking down at its inner surface.

They shot over a mountain range, and a vast plain spread out before them. Here and there, in the far distance, they could see darker spots caused by buckled geological strata.

Arcot swung the ship around, and they saw the vast horizon swing about them as their sensation of "down" changed with the acceleration of the turn. They felt nearly weightless, for they were lifting again in a high arc.

Arcot was heading back toward the mountains they had passed over. He dropped the ship again, and the foothills seemed to rise to meet them.

"I'm heading for that lake," Arcot explained. "It seems absolutely deserted, and there are some things we want to do. I haven't had any decent exercise for the past two weeks, except for straining under high gravity. I want to do some swimming, and we need to distill some water for drink; we need to refill the tanks in case of emergencies. If the atmosphere contains oxygen, fine; if it doesn't, we can get it out of the water by electrolysis.

"But I hope that air is good to breathe, because I've been wanting a swim and a sun bath for a long time!"

XIII

THE *Ancient Mariner* hung high in the air, poised twenty-five miles above the surface of the little lake. Wade, as chemist, tested the air while the others readied the distillation and air condensation apparatus. By the time they had finished, Wade was ready with his report.

"Air pressure about 20 psi at the surface; temperature around ninety-five Fahrenheit. Composition: eighteen percent oxygen, seventy-five percent nitrogen, four-tenths of one percent carbon dioxide, residue—inert gasses. That's not including water vapor, of which there is a fair amount.

"I put a canary into the air, and the bird liked it, so I imagine it's quite safe except for bacteria, perhaps. Naturally, at this altitude the air is germ-free."

"Good," said Morey, "then we can take our swim and work without worrying about spacesuits."

"Just a minute!" Fuller objected. "What about those germs Wade mentioned? If you think I'm going out in my shorts where some flock of bacteria can get at my tender anatomy, you've got another think coming!"

"I wouldn't worry about it," Wade said. "The chances of organisms developing along the same evolutionary line is quite slim. We may find the inhabitants of the same shape as those of another world, because the human body is fairly well constructed anatomically. The head is in a place where it will be able to see over a wide area and it's in a safe place. The hand is very useful and can be improved upon but little. True, the Venerians have a second thumb, but the principle is the same.

"But chemically, the bodies are probably very different. The people of Venus are widely different chemically; the bacteria that can make a Venerian deathly ill is killed the instant it enters our body, or else it starves to death because it can't find the kind of chemical food it needs to live. And the same thing happens when a Venerian is attacked by an Earthly microorganism.

"Even on Earth, evolution has produced such widely varying types of life that an organism that can feed on one is totally incapable of feeding on another. You, for instance, couldn't catch tobacco mosaic virus, and the tobacco plant can't catch the measles virus.

"You couldn't expect a microorganism to evolve here that was capable of feeding on Earth-type tissues; they would have starved to death long ago."

"What about bigger animals?" Fuller asked cautiously.

"That's different. You would probably be indigestible to an alien carnivore, but he'd probably kill you first to find out. If he ate you, it might kill him in the end, but that would be small consolation. That's why we're going to go out armed."

Arcot dropped the ship swiftly until they were hovering a bare hundred feet over the waters of the lake. There was a little stream winding its way down the mountainside, and another which led the clear overflow away.

"I doubt if there's anything of great size in that lake," Arcot said slowly and thoughtfully. "Still, even small fish might be deadly. Let's play safe and remove all forms of life, bacterial and otherwise. A little touch of the molecular motion ray, greatly diffused, will do the trick."

Since the molecular ray directed the motion of the molecules of matter, it prevented chemical reactions from taking place, even when greatly diffused; all the molecules tend to go in the same direction to such an extent that the delicate balance of chemical reactions that is life is upset. It is too delicate a thing to stand any power that upsets the reactions so violently. All things are killed instantly.

As the light haze of the ionized air below them glowed

out in a huge cone, the water of the lake heaved and seemed to move in its depths, but there was no great movement of the waters; they lost only a fraction of their weight. But every living thing in that lake died instantly.

Arcot turned the ship, and the shining hull glided softly over to one side of the lake where a little sandy beach invited them. There seemed no indication of intelligent life about.

Each of them took a load of the supplies they had brought, and carried them out under the shade of an immense pine-like tree—a gigantic column of wood that stretched far into the sky to lose its green leaves in a waving sea of foliage. The mottled sunlight of the bright star above them made them feel very much at home. Its color, intensity, and warmth were all exactly the same as on Earth.

Each of the men wore his power suit to aid in carrying the things they had brought, for the gravity here was a bit higher than that of Earth. The difference in air pressure was so little as to be scarcely noticeable; they even adjusted the interior of the ship to it.

They had every intention of staying here for awhile. It was pleasant to lie in the warm sun once more; so pleasant that it became difficult to remember that they were countless trillions of long miles from their own home planet. It was hard to realize that the warm, blazing star above them was not Old Sol.

Arcot was carrying a load of food in a box. He had neutralized his weight until, load and all, he weighed about a hundred pounds. This was necessary in order to permit him to drag a length of hose behind him toward the water, so it could be used as an intake for the pumps.

Morey, meanwhile, was having trouble. He had been carrying a load of assorted things to use—a few pneumatic pillows, a heavy iron pot for boiling the water, and a number of other things.

He reached his destination, having floated the hundred or so feet from the ship by using his power suit. He forgot, momentarily, and dropped his load. Immediately, he too began to "drop"—upward! He had a buoyancy of around three hundred pounds, and a weight of only two fifty. In dropping the load, the sudden release had caused the power unit to jerk him upward, and somehow the controlling knob on the power pack was torn loose.

Morey shot up into the air, showing a fair rate of progress toward his late abode—space! And he had no way to stop himself. His hand power unit was far too weak to overcome the pull of his power-pack, and he was rising faster and faster!

He realized that his friends could catch him, and laughingly called down: "Arcot! Help! I'm being kidnapped by my power suit! To the rescue!"

Arcot looked up quickly at Morey's call and realized immediately that his power control had come off. He knew there was twenty miles or so of breathable air above, and long before Morey rose that far, he could catch him in the *Ancient Mariner,* if necessary.

He turned on his own power suit, using a lift of a hundred pounds, which gave him double Morey's acceleration. Quickly he gathered speed that shot him up toward his helpless friend, and a moment later, he had caught up with him and passed him. Then he shut off his power and drifted to a halt before he began to drop again. As Morey rose toward him, Arcot adjusted the power in his own suit to match Morey's velocity.

Arcot grabbed Morey's leg and turned his power down until he had a weight of fifty pounds. Soon they were both falling again, and when their rate of fall amounted to approximately twenty miles per hour, Arcot cut their weight to zero and they continued down through their momentum. Just short of the ground, he leaped free of Morey, who, carried on by momentum, touched the ground a moment later. Wade at once jumped in and held him down.

"Now, now! Calm yourself," said Wade solicitously. "Don't go up in the air like that over the least little thing."

"I won't, if you'll get busy and take this damned thing

109

off—or fasten some lead to my feet!" replied Morey, starting to unstrap the mechanism.

"You'd better hold your horses there," said Arcot. "If you take that off now, we sure will need the *Ancient Mariner* to catch up with it. It will produce an acceleration that no man could ever stand—something on the order of five thousand gravities, if the tubes could stand it. And since that one is equipped with the invisibility apparatus, you'd be out one good invisibility suit. Restrain yourself, boy, and I'll go get a new knob control.

"Wade, get the boy a rock to hold him down. Better tie it around his neck so he won't forget it and fly off into space again. It's a nuisance locating so small an object in space and I promised his father I'd bring the body back if there was anything left of it." He released Morey as Wade handed him a large stone.

A few minutes later, he returned with a new adjustment dial and repaired Morey's apparatus. The strain was released when he turned it, and Morey parted with the rock with relief.

Morey grunted in relief, and looked at the offending pack.

"You know, that being stuck with a sky-bound gadget that you can't turn off is the nastiest combination of feeling stupid, helpless, comical, silly and scared I've hit yet. It now—somewhat late—occurs to me that this is powered with a standard power coil, straight off the production line, and that it has a standard overload cut-out for protection of associated equipment. I want to install an emergency cut-off switch, in case a knob, or something else, goes sour. But I want to have the emergency overload where I can decide whether or not an emergency overload is to be accepted. I'd feel a sight more than silly if that overload relay popped while I was a couple thousand feet up.

"Trouble with all this new stuff of ours is that we simply haven't had time to find out all the 'I never thought of that' things that can go wrong. If the grid resistor on that oscillator went out, for instance, what would it do?"

Arcot cocked an eye at the power pack, visualizing the circuits. "Full blast, straight up, and no control. But modern printed resistors don't fail."

"That's what it says in all the books." Wade nodded wisely. "And you should see the stock of replacement units every electronics shop stocks for purposes of replacing infallible units, too. You've got a point, my friend."

"I can see four ways we can change these things to failsafe operation, if we add Morey's emergency cut-off switch. If it did go on-full then, you could use intermittent operation and get down," Arcot acknowledged.

"Anybody know what silly fail-unsafe tricks we overlooked in the *Ancient Mariner?*" Fuller asked.

"That," said Wade with a grimace, "is a silly question. The 'I didn't think of that' type of failure occurs because I didn't think of that, and the reason I didn't think of it is because it never occurred to me. If we'd been able to think of 'em, we would have. We'll probably get stuck with a few more yet, before we get back. But at least we can clean up a few bugs in these things now."

"Forget it for now, Wade, and get that chow on," suggested Fuller. He was lying on his back, clad only in a pair of short trunks, completely relaxed and enjoying life. "We can do that when it's dark here."

"Fuller has the right idea," said Morey, looking at Fuller with a judicious eye. "I think I'll follow his example."

"Which makes three in favor and one on the way," said Arcot, as he came out of the ship and sank lown on the soft sand of the beach.

They lay around for a while after lunch, and then decided to swim in the cool waters of the lake. One of them was to stand guard while the others went in swimming. Standing guard consisted of lying on his back on the soft sand, and staring up at the delightful contrast of lush green foliage and deep blue sky.

It was several hours before they gathered up their things and returned to the ship. They felt more rested than they had before their exercise. They had not been tired before,

111

merely restless, and the physical exercise had made them far more comfortable.

They gathered again in the control room. All the apparatus had been taken in; the tanks were filled, and the compressed oxygen replenished. They closed the airlock and were ready to start again.

As they lifted into the air, Arcot looked at the lake that was shrinking below them. "Nice place for a picnic; we'll have to remember that place. It isn't more than twenty million light years from home."

"Yes," agreed Morey, "it is handy. But suppose we find out where home is first; let's go find the local inhabitants."

"Excellent idea. Which way do we go to look?" Wade asked.

"This lake must have an outlet to the sea," Morey answered. "I suggest we follow it. Most rivers of any size have a port near the mouth, and a port usually means a city."

"Let's go," said Arcot, swinging the shining ship about and heading smoothly down along the line of the little stream that had its beginning at the lake. They moved on across the mountains and over the green foothills until they came to a broad, rolling plain.

"I wonder if this planet *is* inhabited," Arcot mused. "None of this land seems to be cultivated."

Morey had been scanning the horizon with a pair of powerful binoculars. "No, the land isn't cultivated, but take a look over there—see that range of little hills over to the right? Take a look." He handed the binoculars to Arcot.

Arcot looked long and quietly. At last he lowered the binoculars and handed them to Wade, who sat next to him.

"It looks like the ruins of a city," Arcot said. "Not the ruins that a storm would make, but the ruins that high explosives would make. I'd say there had been a war and the people who once lived here had been driven off."

"So would I," rejoined Morey. "I wonder if we could find the conquerors?"

"Maybe—unless it was mutual annihilation!"

They rose a bit higher and raised their speed to a thousand miles an hour. On and on they flew, high above the gently rolling plain, mile after mile. The little brooklet became a great river, and the river kept growing more and more. Ahead of them was a range of hills, and they wondered how the river could thread its way among them. They found that it went through a broad pass that twisted tortuously between high mountains.

A few miles farther on, they came to a great natural basin in the pass, a wide, level bowl. And in almost the exact center, they saw a looming mass of buildings—a great city!

"Look!" cried Morey. "I told you it was inhabited!"

Arcot winced. "Yes, but if you shout in my ear like that again, you'll have to write things out for me for ever after." He was just as excited as Morey, nevertheless.

The great mass of the city was shaped like a titanic cone that stood half mile high and was fully a mile and a half in radius. But the remarkable thing about it was the perfect uniformity with which the buildings and every structure seemed to conform to this plan. It seemed as though an invisible, but very tangible line had been drawn in the air.

It was as though a sign had been posted: "Here there shall be buildings. Beyond this line, no structure shall extend, nor any vehicle go!"

The air directly above the city was practically packed with slim, long, needle-like ships of every size—from tiny private ships less than fifteen feet long to giant freighters of six hundred feet and longer. And every one of them conformed to the rule perfectly!

Only around the base of the city there seemed to be a slight deviation. Where the invisible cone should have touched the ground, there was a series of low buildings made of some dark metal, and all about them the ground appeared scarred and churned.

"They certainly seem to have some kind of ray screen over that city," Morey commented. "Just look at that perfect cone effect and those low buildings are undoubtedly the projectors."

Arcot had brought the ship to a halt as he came through

the pass in the mountain. The shining hull was in the cleft of the gorge, and was, no doubt, quite hard to see from the city.

Suddenly, a vagrant ray of the brilliant sun reached down through a break in the overcast of clouds and touched the shining hull of the *Ancient Mariner* with a finger of gold. Instantly, the ship shone like the polished mirror of a heliograph.

Almost immediately, a low sound came from the distant city. It was a pulsing drone that came through the microphone in a weird cadence; a low, beating drone, like some wild music. Louder and stronger it grew, rising in pitch slowly, then it suddenly ended in a burst of rising sound— a terrific whoop of alarm.

As if by magic, every ship in the air above the city shot downward, dropping suddenly out of sight. In seconds, the air was cleared.

"It seems they've spotted us," said Arcot in a voice he tried to make nonchalant.

A fleet of great, long ships was suddenly rising from the neighborhood of the central building, the tallest of the group. They went in a compact wedge formation and shot swiftly down along the wall of the invisible cone until they were directly over the low building nearest the *Ancient Mariner*. There was a sudden shimmer in the air. In an instant, the ships were through and heading toward the *Ancient Mariner* at a tremendous rate.

They shot forward with an acceleration that was astonishing to the men in the spaceship. In perfect formation, they darted toward the lone, shining ship from far-off Earth!

XIV

THE FOUR EARTHMEN watched the fleet of alien ships roar through the air toward them.

"Now how shall we signal them?" asked Morey, also trying to be nonchalant, and failing as badly as Arcot had.

"Don't try the light beam method," cautioned Arcot. The last time they had tried to use a light beam signal was when they first contacted the Nigrans. The Nigrans thought it was some kind of destruction ray. That had started the terrible destructive war of the Black Star.

"Let's just hang here peaceably and see what they do," Arcot suggested.

Motionless, the *Ancient Mariner* hung before the advancing attack of the great battle fleet. The shining hull was a thing of beauty in the golden sunlight as it waited for the advancing ships.

The alien ships 'slowed as they approached and spread out in a great fan-shaped crescent.

Suddenly, the *Ancient Mariner* gave a tremendous leap and hurtled toward them at a terrific speed, under an acceleration so great that Arcot was nearly hurled into unconsciousness. He would have been except for the terrific mass of the ship. To produce that acceleration in so great a mass, a tremendous force was needed, a force that even made the enemy fleet reel under its blow!

But, sudden as it was, Arcot had managed to push the power into reverse, using the force of the molecular drive to counteract the attraction the aliens had brought to bear.

The whole mighty fabric of the ship creaked as the titanic load came upon it. They were using a force of a million tons!

The mighty lux beams withstood the stress, however, and the ship came to a halt, then was swiftly backing away from the alien battle fleet.

"We can give them all they want!" said Arcot grimly. He noticed that Wade and Fuller had been knocked out by the sudden blow, but Morey, though slightly groggy, was still in possession of his senses.

"Let's not," Morey remonstrated. "We may be able to make friends with them, but not if we kill them off."

"Right!" replied Arcot, "but we're going to give them a little demonstration of power!"

The *Ancient Mariner* leaped suddenly upward with a speed that defied the eyes of the men at the rays of the enemy ships. Then, as they turned to follow the sudden motion of the ship—*it was not there!*

The *Ancient Mariner* had vanished!

Morey was startled for an instant as the ship and his companions disappeared around him, then he realized what had happened. Arcot had used the invisibility apparatus!

Arcot turned and raced swiftly far off to one side, behind the strange ships, and hovered over the great cliff that made the edge of the cleft that was the river bed. Then he snapped the ship into full visibility.

Wade and Fuller had recovered by now, and Arcot started barking out orders. "Wade—Fuller—take the molecular ray, Wade, and tear down that cliff—throw it down into the valley. Fuller, turned the heat beams on with all the power you can get and burn that refuse he tears down into a heap of molten lava!

"I'm going to show them what we can do! And, Wade— after Fuller gets it melted down, throw the molten lava high in the air!"

From the ship, a long pencil of rays, faintly violet from the air they ionized, reached out and touched the cliff. In an instant, it had torn down a vast mass of the solid rock, which came raining down into the valley with a roaring thunder and threw the dirt of the valley into the air like splashed mud.

Then the violet ray died, and two rays of blinding brilliance reached out. The rock was suddenly smoking, steaming. Then it became red, dull at first, then brighter and brighter. Suddenly it collapsed into a great pool of white-hot lava, flowing like water under the influence of the beams from the ship.

Again the pale violet of the molecular beams touched the rock—which was now bubbling lava. In an instant, the great mass of flaming incandescent rock was flying like a glowing meteor, up into the air. It shot up with terrific speed, broke up in mid-air, and fell back as a rain of red-hot stone.

The bright rays died out, but the pale fingers of the molecular beams traced across the level ground. As they touched it, the solid soil spouted into the air like some vast fountain, to fall back as frost-covered powder.

The rays that had swung a sun into destruction were at work! What chance had man, or the works of man against such? What mattered a tiny planet when those rays could hurl one mighty sun into another, to blaze up in an awful conflagration that would light up space for a million light years around with a mighty glare of light!

As if by a giant plow, the valley was torn and rent in great streaks by the pale violet rays of the molecular force. Wade tore loose a giant builder and sent it rocketing into the heavens. It came down with a terrific crash minutes later, to bury itself deep in the soil as it splintered into fragments.

Suddenly the *Ancient Mariner* was jerked violently again. Evidently undaunted by their display of power, the aliens' rays had gripped the Earthmen's ship again and were drawing it with terrific acceleration. But this time the ship was racing toward the city, caught by the beam of one of the low-built, sturdy buildings that housed the protective ray projectors.

Again Arcot threw on the mighty power units that drove the ship, bracing them against the pull of the beam.

"Wade! Use the molecular ray! Stop that beam!" Arcot ordered.

The ship was stationary, quivering under the titanic forces that struggled for it. The enemy fleet raced toward them, trying to come to the aid of the men in the tower.

The pale glow of the molecular beam reached out its ghostly finger and touched the heavy-walled ray projector building. There was a sudden flash of discharging energy, and the tower was hurled high in the air, leaving only a gaping hole in the ground.

Instantly, with the collapse of the beam that held it, the *Ancient Mariner* shot backward, away from the scene of the battle. Arcot snapped off the drive and turned on the invisibility apparatus. They hung motionless, silent and invisible in the air, awaiting developments.

In close formation, one group of ships blocked the opening in the wall of rays that the removal of one projector building had caused. Three other ships went to investigate the wreck of the building that had fallen a mile away.

The rest of the fleet circled the city, darting around, searching frantically for the invisible enemy, fully aware of the danger of collision. The unnerving tension of expecting it every second made them erratic and nervous to the nth degree.

"They're sticking pretty close to home," said Arcot. "They don't seen to be too anxious to play with us."

"They don't, do they?" Morey said, looking angry. "They might at least have been willing to see what we wanted. I want to investigate some other cities. Come on!" He had thoroughly enjoyed the rest at the little mountain lake, and he was disappointed that they had been driven away. Had they wanted to, he knew, they could easily have torn the entire city out by the roots!

"I think we ought to smash them thoroughly," said Wade. "They're certainly inhospitable people!"

"And I, for one, would like to know what that attraction ray was," said Fuller curiously.

"The ray is easily understood after you take a look at

the wreck it made of some of these instruments," Arcot told him. "It was projected magnetism. I can see how it might be done if you worked on it for a while. The ray simply attracted everything in its path that was magnetic, which included our lux metal hull.

"Luckily, most of our apparatus is shielded against magnetism. The few things that aren't can be repaired easily. But I'll bet Wade finds his gear in the galley thrown around quite a bit."

"Where do we go from here, then?" Wade asked.

"Well, this world is bigger than Earth," said Morey. "Even if they're afraid to go out of their cities to run farms, they must have other cities. The thing that puzzles me, though, is how they do it—I don't see how they can possibly raise enough food for a city in the area they have available!"

" 'People couldn't possibly live in hydrogen instead of oxygen'," Arcot quoted, grinning. "That's what they told me when I made my little announcement at the meeting on the Black Star situation. The only trouble was—they did. That suggestion of yours meets the same fate, Morey!"

"All right, you win," agreed Morey. "Now let's see if we can find the other nations on this world more friendly."

Arcot looked at the sun. "We're now well north of the equator. We'll go up where the air is thin, put on some speed, and go into the south temperate zone. We'll see if we can't find some people there who are more peaceably inclined."

Arcot cut off the invisibility tubes. Instantly, all the enemy ships in the neighborhood turned and darted toward them at top speed. But the shining *Ancient Mariner* darted into the deep blue vault of the sky, and a moment later was lost to their view.

"They had a lot of courage," said Arcot, looking down at the city as it sank out of sight. "It doesn't take one-quarter as much courage to fight a known enemy, no matter how deadly, as it does to fight a known enemy force—something that can tear down mountains and throw their forts into the air like toys."

119

"Oh, they had courage, all right," Morey conceded, "but I wish they hadn't been quite so anxious to display it!"

They were high above the ground now, accelerating with a force of one gravity. Arcot cut the acceleration down until there was just enough to overcome the air resistance, which, at the height they were flying, was very low. The sky was black above them, and the stars were showing around the blazing sun. They were unfamiliar stars in unfamiliar constellations—the stars of another universe.

In a very short time, the ship was dropping rapidly downward again, the horizontal power off. The air resistance slowed them rapidly. They drifted high over the south temperate zone. Below them stretched the seemingly endless expanse of a great blue-green ocean.

"They don't lack for water, do they?" Wade commented.

"We could pretty well figure on large oceans," Arcot said. "The land is green, and there are plenty of clouds."

Far ahead, a low mass of solid land appeared above the blue of the horizon. It soon became obvious that it was not a continent they were approaching, but a large island, stretching hundreds of miles north and south.

Arcot dropped the ship lower; the mountainous terrain had become so broken that it would be impossible to detect a city from thirty miles up.

The green defiles of the great mountains not only provided good camouflage, but kept any great number of ships from attacking the sides, where the ray stations were. The cities were certainly located with an eye for war! Arcot wondered what sort of conflict had lasted so long that cities were designed for perpetual war. Had they never had peace?

"Look!" Fuller called. "There's another city!" Below them, situated in a little natural bowl in the mountains, was another of the cone cities.

Wade and Fuller manned the ray projectors again; Arcot dropped the ship toward the city, one hand on the *reverse* switch in case the inhabitants tried to use the magnetic beam again.

At last, they had come quite low. There were no ships in the air, and no people in sight.

Suddenly, the outside microphone picked up a low, humming sound. A long, cigar-shaped object was heading toward the ship at high speed. It had been painted a dark, mottled green, and was nearly invisible against background of foliage beneath the ship.

"Wade! Catch that on the ray!" Arcot commanded sharply, moving the ship to one side at the same time. Instantly, the guided missile turned and kept coming toward them.

Wade triggered the molecular beam, and the missile was suddenly dashing toward the ground with terrific speed. There was a terrific flash of flame and a shock wave of concussion. A great hole gaped in the ground.

"They sure know their chemistry," remarked Wade, looking down at the great hole the explosion had torn in the ground. "That wasn't atomic, but on the other hand, it wasn't dynamite or TNT, either! I'd like to know what they use!"

"Personally," said Arcot angrily, "I think that was more or less a gentle hint to move on!" He didn't like the way they were being received; he had wanted to meet these people. Of course, the other planet might be inhabited, but if it wasn't—

"I wonder—" said Morey thoughtfully. "Arcot, those people were obviously warned against our attack—probably by that other city. Now, we've come nearly halfway around this world; certainly we couldn't have gone much farther away and still be on the planet. And we find this city in league with the other! Since this league goes halfway around the world, and they expected us to do the same, isn't it fair to assume, just on the basis of geographical location, that all this world is in one league?"

"Hmmm—an interplanetary war," mused Arcot. "That would certainly prove that one of the other planets is inhabited. The question is—which one?"

"The most probable one is the next inner planet, Aphrodite," replied Morey.

Arcot fired the ship into the sky. "If your conclusions are correct—and I think they are—I see no reason to stay on this planet. Let's go see if their neighbors are less aggressive!"

With that, he shot the ship straight up, rotating the axis until it was pointing straight away from the planet. He increased the acceleration until, as they left the outer fringes of the atmosphere, the ship was hitting a full four gravities.

"I'm going to shorten things up and use the space control," Arcot said. "The gravitational field of the sun will drain a lot of our energy out, but so what? Lead is cheap, and before we're through, we'll have plenty or I'll know the reason why!"

Dr. Richard Arcot was angry—boiling all the way through!

XV

THERE WAS THE familiar tension in the air as the space field built up and they were hurled suddenly forward; the star-like dot of the planet suddenly expanded as they rushed forward at a speed far greater than that of light. In a moment, it had grown to a disc; Arcot stopped the space control. Again they were moving forward on molecular drive.

Very shortly, Arcot began to decelerate. Within ten minutes, they were beginning to feel the outermost wisps of the cloud-laden atmosphere. The heat of the blazing sun was intense; the surface of the planet was, no doubt, a far warmer place than Earthmen would find comfortable. They would have been far better suited to remain on the other planet, but they very evidently were not wanted!

They dropped down through the atmosphere, sinking for

miles as the ship slowed to the retarding influence of the air and the molecular power. Down they went, through mile after mile of heavy cloud layer, unable to see the ground beneath them.

Then, suddenly, the thick, all-enveloping mists that held them were gone. They were flying smoothly along under leaden skies—perpetual, dim, dark clouds. Despite the brightness of the sun above them, the clouds made the light dim and gray. They reflected such an enormous percentage of the light that struck them that the climate was not as hot as they had feared.

The ground was dark under its somber mantle of clouds; the hills, the rivers that crawled across wide plains, and the oddly stunted forests all looked as though they had been modeled in a great mass of greenish-gray putty. It was a discouraging world.

"I'm glad we didn't wait for our swim here," remarked Wade. "It sure looks like rain."

Arcot stopped the ship and held it motionless at ten miles while Wade made his chemical analysis of the air. The report looked favorable; plenty of oxygen and a trace of carbon dioxide mixed with nitrogen.

"But the water vapor!" Wade said. "The air is saturated with it! It won't be the heat, but the humidity that'll bother us—to coin a phrase."

Arcot dropped the ship still farther, at the same time moving forward toward a sea he had seen in the distance. Swiftly, the ground sped beneath them. The low plain sloped toward the sea, a vast, level surface of gray, leaden water.

"Oh, brother, what a pleasant world," said Fuller sarcastically.

It was certainly not an inspiring scene. The leaden skies, the heavy clouds, the dark land, and the gray-green of the sea, always shaded in perpetual half-light, lest the burning sun heat them beyond endurance. It was a gloomy world.

They turned and followed the coast. Still no sign of inhabitants was visible. Mile after mile passed beneath them as the shining ship followed up the ragged shore. Small indentations and baylets ran into a shallow, level sea. This world had no moon, so it was tideless, except for the slight solar tides.

Finally, far ahead of them, and well back from the coast, Arcot spotted a great mountain range.

"I'm going to head for that," he told the others. "If these people are at war with our very inimical friends of the other planet, chances are they'll put their cities in the mountains, too."

They had such cities. The *Ancient Mariner* had penetrated less than a hundred miles along the twisted ranges of the mountains before they saw, far ahead, a great, cone-shaped city. The city was taller, larger than those of the other planet, and the cone ran up farther from the actual city buildings, leaving the aircraft more room.

Arcot stopped and watched the city a long time through the telescope. It seemed similar to the others in all respects. The same type of needle-like ships floated in the air above it, and the same type of cone ray projectors nestled in the base of the city's invisible protection.

"We may as well take a chance," said Arcot. He shot the ship forward until they were within a mile of the city, in plain sight of the inhabitants.

Suddenly, without any warning signal, apparently, all the air traffic went wild—then it was gone. Every ship seemed to have ducked into some unseen place of refuge.

Within a few minutes, a fleet of battleships was winging its way toward the invisible barrier. Then it was out, and, in a great semi-cylinder a quarter of a mile high, and a quarter of a mile in radius, they advanced toward the *Ancient Mariner*.

Arcot kept the ship motionless. He knew that their only weapon was the magnetic ray; otherwise they would have won the war long ago. And he knew he could cope with magnetism.

Slowly the ships advanced. At last, they halted a quarter of a mile from the Earth ship. A single ship detached itself from the mass and advanced to within a few hundred feet of the *Ancient Mariner.*

Quickly, Arcot jumped to his feet. "Morey, take the controls. Evidently they want to parley, not fight. I'm going over there."

He ran the length of the corridor to his room and put on his power suit. A moment later, he left the airlock and launched himself into space, flying swiftly toward the ship. He had come alone, but armed as he was, he was probably more than a match for anything they could bring to bear on him.

He went directly toward the broad expanse of glass that marked the control room of the alien ship and looked in curiously.

The pilot was a man much like Arcot; quite tall, and of tremendous girth, with a huge chest and great powerful arms. His hands, like those of the Venerians, had two thumbs.

With equal curiosity, the man stared at Arcot, floating in the air without apparent means of support.

Arcot hung there a moment, then motioned that he wished to enter. The giant alien motioned him around to the side of the ship. Halfway down the length of the ship, Arcot saw a port suddenly open. He flew swiftly forward and entered.

The man who stood there was a giant as tall as Wade and even more magnificently muscled, with tremendous shoulders and giant chest. His thighs, rounded under a close-fitting gray uniform, were bulging with smooth muscle.

He was considerably larger than the man in the pilot room, and whereas the other had been a pale yellow in color, this man was burned to a more healthy shade of tan. His features were regular and pleasing; his hair was black and straight; his high forehead denoted a high degree of intelligence, and his clear black eyes, under heavy black eyebrows, seemed curious, but friendly.

His nose was rather thin, but not sharp, and his mouth was curved in a smile of welcome. His chin was firm and sharp, distinct from his face and neck.

125

They looked each other over, and Arcot smiled as their eyes met.

"Torlos," said the alien, pointing to his great chest.

"Arcot," replied the Earthmen, pointing to himself. Then he pointed to the stranger. "Torlos." He knew he hadn't pronounced it exactly as the alien had, but it would suffice.

The stranger smiled in approval. "Ahcut," he said, pointing to the Earthman.

Then he pointed to the comparatively thin arms of the Earthman, and to his own. Then he pointed to Arcot's head and to the mechanism he wore on his back, then to his own head, and went through the motions of walking with great effort.

Again he pointed at Arcot's head, nodding his own in approval.

Arcot understood immediately what was meant. The alien had indicated that the Earthman was comparatively weak, but that he had no need of muscle, for he made his head and his machines work for him. And he had decided that the head was better!

Arcot looked at the man's eyes and concentrated on the idea of friendship, projecting it with all his mental power. The black eyes suddenly widened in surprise, which quickly turned to pleasure as he tried to concentrate on one thought.

It was difficult for Arcot to interpret the thoughts of the alien; all his concepts were in a different form. At last, he caught the idea of location—but it was location in the interrogative! How was he to interpret that?

Then it hit him. Torlos was asking: "Where are you from?"

Arcot pulled a pad of paper and a pencil from his pocket and began to sketch rapidly. First, he drew the local galaxy, with dots for stars, and swept his hand around him. He made one of the dots a little heavier and pointed at the bright blur in the cloudy sky above them. Then he drew a circle around that dot and put another dot on it, at the same time indicating the planet beneath them.

Torlos showed that he understood.

Arcot continued. At the other end of the paper, he drew

another galaxy, and indicated Earth. Then he drew a dotted line from Earth to the planet they were now on.

Torlos looked at him in incredulous wonder. Again he indicated his respect for Arcot's brain.

Arcot smiled and indicated the city. "Can we go there?" he projected into the other's mind.

Torlos turned and glanced toward the end of the corridor. There was no one in sight, so he shouted an order in a deep, pleasant voice. Instantly, another giant man came striding down the corridor with a lithe softness that indicated tremendous muscular power, excellently controlled. He saluted by placing his left hand over the right side of his chest. Arcot noted that for future reference.

Torlos spoke to the other alien for a moment. The other left and returned a minute later and said something to Torlos. Torlos turned to Arcot indicating that he should return to his ship and follow them.

Arcot suddenly turned his eyes and looked directly into the black eyes of the alien. "Torlos," he projected, "will you come with us on our ship?"

"I am commander of this ship. I can not go without the permission of my chief. I will ask my chief."

Again he turned and left Arcot. He was back in a few minutes carrying a small handbag. "I can go. This keeps me in communication with my ship."

Arcot adjusted his weight to zero and floated lightly out the doorway. He rose about six feet above the landing, then indicated to Torlos that he was to grasp Arcot's feet, one in each hand. Torlos closed a grip of steel about each ankle and stepped off the platform.

At once, they dropped, for the power suit had not been adjusted to the load. Arcot yelped in pain as Torlos, in his surprise at not floating, involuntarily gripped tighter. Quickly, Arcot turned on more power and gasped as he felt the weight mount swiftly. He had estimated Torlos' weight at two hundred seventy or so—and it was more like three hundred and fifty! Soon, however, he had the weight adjusted, and they floated easily up toward the *Ancient Mariner*.

They floated in through the door of the ship, and, once inside, Torlos released his hold. Arcot was immediately slammed to the roof with a weight of three hundred and fifty pounds!

A moment later, he was again back on the floor, rubbing his back. He shook his head and frowned, then smiled and pretended to limp.

"Don't let go so suddenly," he admonished telepathically.

"I did not know. I am sorry," Torlos thought contritely.

"Who's your friend?" asked Wade as he entered the corridor. "He certainly looks husky."

"He is," Arcot affirmed. "And he must be weighted with lead! I thought he'd pull my legs off. Look at those arms!"

"I don't want to get him mad at me," Wade grinned. "He looks like he'd make a mean opponent. What's his name?"

"Torlos," replied Arcot, just as Fuller stepped in.

Torlos was looking curiously at a crowbar that had been lying in a rack on the wall. He picked it up and flexed it a bit, as a man might flex a rapier to test its material. Then he held it far out in front of him and proceeded to tie a knot in the inch-thick metal bar! Then, still frowning in puzzlement, he untied it, straightened it as best he could, and put it back in the rack.

The Earthmen were staring in utter astonishment to see the terrific strength the man displayed.

He smiled as he turned to them again.

"If he could do that at arm's length," Wade said thoughtfully, "what could he do if he really tried?"

"Why don't you try and see?" Fuller asked sweetly.

"I can think of easier—but probably no quicker—ways of committing suicide," Wade replied.

Arcot laughed and, looking at Torlos, projected the general meaning of the last remarks. Torlos joined them in the laugh.

"All my people are strong," he thought. "I can not understand why you are not. That was a tool? We could not use it so; it is too weak."

Wade and the others picked up the thought, and Wade

128

laughed. "I suppose they use old I-beams to tie up their Christmas presents."

Arcot held a moment of silent consultation with Torlos, then turned to the others. "We are supposed to follow these men to their city to have some kind of an audience with their ruler, according to Torlos. Let's get started; the rest of the fleet is waiting."

Arcot led Torlos through the main engine room, and was going into the main coil room when Torlos stopped him.

"Is this all your drive apparatus?" he thought.

"Yes, it is," Arcot projected.

"It is smaller than the power equipment of a small private machine!" His thoughts radiated surprise. "How could you make so great a distance?"

"Power," said Arcot. "Look!" He drew his molecular ray pistol. "This alone is powerful enough to destroy all your battle fleet without any danger on our part. And, despite your strength, you are helpless against me!"

Arcot touched a switch on his belt and vanished.

In amazement, Torlos reached out a hand to the spot where Arcot had stood. There was nothing there. Suddenly, he turned, touching the back of his head. Something had tugged at his hair!

He looked all around him and moved his arms around—to no avail. There was nothing there.

Then, in the blink of an eye, Arcot was floating in the air before him. "What avails strength against air, Torlos?" he asked, smiling.

"For safety's sake," Torlos thought, "I want to be your friend!" He grinned widely.

Arcot led the way on into the control room, where Morey had already started to follow the great fleet toward the city.

"What are we going to do at the city?" Arcot asked Torlos telepathically.

"This is the capital of the world, Sator, and here is the commander-of-all-military-and-civil-forces. It is he you will see. He has been summoned," Torlos replied carefully.

"We visited the third world of this system first," Arcot

129

told the alien, "and they repulsed us. We tried to be friendly, but they attacked us at once. In order to keep from being
damaged, we had to destroy one of their city-protecting ray
buildings." This last thought was hard to transmit; Arcot
had pictured mentally a scene in which the ray building was
ripped out of the ground and hurled into the air.

In sudden anxiety and concern, Torlos stared into Arcot's
eyes. And in that look, Arcot read what even telepathy had
hidden heretofore.

"Did you destroy the city?" asked Torlos anxiously. But
it was not the question of a man hoping for the destruction
of his enemies' cities; Arcot got the mental picture of the
city, but with it, he picked up the idea of "home"! Of
course, the ideas of "city" and "home" might be synonymous
with these people; they never seemed to leave their cities.
But why this feeling of worry?

"No, we didn't want to hurt them," Arcot thought. "We
destroyed the ray building only in self defense."

"I understand." Despite obvious mental efforts, Torlos
positively radiated a feeling of relief!

"Are you at war with that world?" Arcot asked coolly.

"The two worlds have been at war for many genera-
tions," Torlos said, then quickly changed the subject. "You
will soon meet the leader of all the forces of Sator. He is
all-powerful here. His word must be absolutely obeyed. It
would be wise if you did not unnecessarily offend him. I see
from what your mind tells me that you have great power, but
there are many ships on Sator, more than Nansal can boast.

"Our commander, Horlan, is a military commander, but
since every man is necessarily a soldier, he is a true ruler."

"I understand," Arcot thought. He turned to Morey and
spoke in English, which Torlos could not understand. "Morey, we're going to see the top man here. He rules the army,
which runs everything. You and I will go, and leave Wade
and Fuller behind as a rear guard. It may not be dangerous, but after being chased off one world, we ought to be
as careful as possible.

"We'll go fully armed, and we'll stay in radio contact at

all times. Watch yourselves; we don't want them even to touch this ship until we know what kind of people they are."

They had followed the Satorian ships toward the city. The giant magnetic ray barrier opened for them, and the *Ancient Mariner* followed. They were inside the alien city.

XVI

BELOW THE *Ancient Mariner*, the great buildings of the alien city jutted up in the gray light of this gray world; their massiveness seemed only to accentuate the depressing light.

On the broad roofs, they saw hundreds of people coming out to watch them as they moved across the city. According to Torlos, they were the first friendly strangers they had ever seen. They had explored all the planets of this system without finding friendly life.

The buildings sloped up toward the center of the city, and the mass of the great central building loomed before them.

The fleet that was leading the Earth ship settled down to a wide courtyard that surrounded the building. Arcot dropped the *Ancient Mariner* down beside them. The men from Torlos' ship formed into two squads as they came out of the airlocks and marched over to the great shining ship of Earth. They formed two neat rows, one on each side of the airlock.

"Come on, Morey," said Arcot. "We're wanted. Wade, keep the radio going at full amplification; the building may cut out some of the power. I'll try to keep you posted on what's going on, but we'll probably be busy answering questions telepathically."

Arcot and Morey followed Torlos out into the dim light of the gray sky, walking across the courtyard between the ranks of the soldiers from Torlos' ship.

Before them was a heavy gate of solid bronze which swung on massive bronze hinges. The building seemed to be made of a dense, gray stone, much like granite, which was depressing in its perfectly unrelieved front. There were no bright spots of color as there were on all Earthly and Venerian structures. Even the lines were grimly utilitarian; there seemed to be no decoration.

Through the great bronze door they walked, and across a small vestibule. Then they were in a mighty concourse, a giant hallway that went completely through the structure. All around them great granite pillars rose to support the mighty building above. Square cut, they lent but little grace to the huge room, but the floor and walls were made of a hard, light green stone, almost the same color as foliage.

On one wall there was a giant tablet, a great plaque fifteen feet high, made of a deep violet stone, and inlaid with a series of characters in the language of this world. Like English letters, they seemed to read horizontally, but whether they read from left to right or right to left there was no way of knowing. The letters themselves were made of some red metal which Arcot and Morey didn't recognize.

Arcot turned to Torlos and projected a thought: "What is that tablet?"

"Ever since the beginning of the war with the other planet, Nansal, the names of our mighty leaders have been inscribed on that plaque in the rarest metal."

The term "rarest metal" was definite to Torlos, and Arcot decided to question him further on the meaning of it when time permitted.

They crossed the great hall and came to what was evidently an elevator. The door slid open, and the two Earthmen followed Torlos and his lieutenant into the cubicle. Torlos pushed a small button. The door slid shut, and a moment later, Arcot and Morey staggered under the sudden terrific load as the car shot upward under an acceleration of at least three gravities!

It continued just long enough for the Earthmen to get used to it, then it snapped off, and they went flying up toward the ceiling as it continued upward under its own momentum. It slowed under the influence of the planet's gravitation and came to a stop exactly opposite the doorway of a higher floor.

"Wow! Some elevator!" exclaimed Morey as he stepped out, flexing his knees as he tried to readjust himself. "That's what I call a violent way of getting upstairs! It wasn't designed by a lazy man or a cripple! I prefer to walk, thanks! What I want to know is how the old people get upstairs. Or do they die young from using their elevators?"

"No," mused Arcot. "That's the funny thing. They don't seem to be bothered by the acceleration. They actually jumped a little off the floor when we started, and didn't seem to experience much difficulty when we stopped." He looked thoughtful for a moment. "You know, when Torlos was bending that crowbar back there in the ship, I picked up a curious thought—I wonder if—" He turned to the giant alien. "Torlos, you once gave me the thought-idea 'bone metal'; what is that?"

Torlos looked at him in surprise and then pointed mutely to a heavy belt he wore—made of closely woven links of iron wire!

"I was right, Morey!" Arcot exclaimed. "These men have *iron bones!* No wonder he could bend that crowbar! It would be as easy as it would for you or me to snap a human arm bone!"

"But, wait a minute!" Morey objected. "How could iron grow?"

"How can stone grow?" countered Arcot. "That's what your bones are, essentially—calcium phosphate rock! It's just a matter of different body chemistry. Their body fluids are probably alkaline, and iron won't rust in an alkaline solution." Arcot was talking rapidly as they followed the aliens down the long corridor.

133

"The thing that confirms my theory is that elevator. It's merely an iron cage in a magnetic beam, and it's pulled up with a terrific acceleration. With iron bones, these men would be similarly influenced, and they wouldn't notice the acceleration so much."

Morey grinned. "I'll be willing to bet they don't use cells in their prisons, here! Just magnetize the floor, and the poor guy could never get away!"

Arcot nodded. "Of course, the bones must be pure iron; their bones evidently don't retain any of the magnetism when they leave the field."

"We seem to be here," Morey interrupted. "Let's continue the discussion later."

Their party had stopped just outside a large, elaborately carved door, the first sign of ornamentation the Earthmen had seen. There were four guards armed with pistols, which, they discovered later, were powered by compressed air under terrific pressure. They hurled a small metal slug through a rifled barrel, and were effective over a distance of about a mile, although they could only fire four times without reloading.

Torlos spoke briefly with the guard, who saluted and opened the door. The two Earthmen followed Torlos into a large room.

Before them was a large, crescent-shaped table, around which were seated several men. At the center of the crescent curve sat a man in a gray uniform, but he was so bedecked with insignia, medals, ribbons, and decorations that his uniform was scarcely visible.

The entire assemblage, including the leader, rose as the Earthmen entered. Arcot and Morey, taking the hint, snapped to attention and delivered a precise military salute.

"We greet you in the name of our planet," said Arcot aloud. "I know you don't understand a word I'm saying, but I hope it sounds impressive enough. We salute you, O High Muckymuck!"

Morey, successfully keeping a straight face, raised his hand and said sonorously: "That goes double for me, bub."

134

In his own language, the leader replied, putting his hands to his hips with a definite motion, and shaking his head from side to side at the same time.

Arcot watched the man closely while he spoke. He was taller than Torlos, but less heavily built, as were all the others here. It seemed that Torlos was unusually powerful, even for this world.

When the leader had finished, Arcot smiled and turned to project this thoughts at Torlos.

"Tell your leader that we come from a planet far away across the vast depths of space. We come in peace, and we will leave in peace, but we would like to ask some favors of him, which we will repay by giving him the secret of our weapons. With them, he can easily conquer Nansal.

"All we want is some wire made from the element lead and some information from your astronomers."

Torlos turned and spoke to his leader in a deep, powerful voice.

Meanwhile, Morey was trying to get in communication with the ship. The walls, however, seemed to be made of metal, and he couldn't get through to Wade.

"We're cut off from the ship," he said quietly to Arcot.

"I was afraid of that, but I think it'll be all right. Our proposition is too good for them to turn down."

Torlos turned back to Arcot when the leader had finished speaking. "The Commanding One asks that you prove the possibilities of your weapons. His scientists tell him that it is impossible to make the trip that you claim to have made."

"What your scientists say is true, to an extent," Arcot thought. "They have learned that no body can go faster than the speed of light—is that not so?"

"Yes. Such, they say, is the fact. To have made this trip, you must, of necessity, be not less than twenty million years old!"

"Tell them that there are some things they do not yet know about space. The velocity of light is a thing that is fixed by the nature of space, right?"

Torlos consulted with the scientists again, then turned

back to Arcot. "They agree that they do not know all the secrets of the Universe, but they agree that the speed of light is fixed by the nature of space."

"How fast does sound travel?" Arcot asked.

"They ask in what medium do you mean?"

"How fast does light travel? In air? In glass? The speed of light is as variable as that of sound. If I can alter the nature of space, so as to make the velocity of light greater, can I not then go faster than in normal space?"

"They say that this is true," Torlos said, after more conversation with the men at the table, "but they say that space is unalterable, since it is emptiness."

"Ask them if they know of the curvature of space." Arcot was becoming worried for fear his explanation would be unintelligible; unless they knew his terms, he could not explain, and it would take a long time to teach them.

"They say," Torlos thought, "that I have misunderstood you. They say space could not possibly be curved, for space is emptiness, and how could empty nothingness be curved."

Arcot turned to Morey and shrugged his shoulders. "I give up, Morey; it's a bad case. If they insist that space is nothing, and can't be curved, I can't go any further."

"If they don't know of the curvature of space," said Morey, "ask them how they learned that the velocity of light is the limiting velocity of a moving body."

Torlos translated and the scientists gave their reply. "They say that you do not know more of space than they, for they know that the speed of light is ultimate. They have tested this with spaceships at high speeds and with experiments with the smallest particles of electricity."

The scientists were looking at Arcot now in protest; they felt he was trying to foist something off on them.

Arcot, too, was becoming exasperated. "Well, if they insist that we couldn't have come from another star, where do they think I come from? They have explored this system and found no such people as we, so I must have come from another star. How? If they won't accept my explanations, let them think up a theory of their own to explain the facts!" He paused for Torlos to translate, then went on. "They say I don't know any more than they do. Tell them to watch this."

He drew his molecular ray pistol and lifted a heavy metal chair into the air. Then Morey drew his heat beam and turned it on the chair. In a few seconds, it was glowing white hot, and then it collapsed into a fiery ball of liquid metal. Morey shut off the heat beam, and Arcot held the ball in the air while it cooled rapidly under the influence of the molecular ray. Then he lowered it to the floor.

It was obvious that the scientists were impressed, and the Emperor was talking eagerly with the men around him. They talked for several minutes, saying nothing to the Earthmen. Torlos stood quietly, waiting for a message to relay.

The Emperor called out, and some of the guards moved inside the door.

Torlos turned to Arcot. "Show no emotion!" came his telepathic warning. "I have been listening to them as they spoke. The Commanding One wants your weapons. Regardless of what his scientists tell him about the possibility of your trip, he knows those weapons work, and he wants them.

"You see, I am not a Satorian at all. I'm from Nansal, sent here many years ago as a spy. I have served in their fleets for many years, and have gained their trust.

"I am telling you the truth, as you will soon see.

"These people are going to follow their usual line of action and take the most direct way toward their end. They are going to attack you, believing that you, despite your weapons, will go down before superior numbers.

"And you'd better move fast; he's calling the guards already!"

Arcot turned to Morey, his face calm, his heart beating like a vibrohammer. "Keep your face straight, Morey. Don't look surprised. They're planning to jump us. We'll rip out the right wall and—"

He stopped. It was too late! The order had been given, and the guards were leaping toward them. Arcot grabbed

137

at his ray pistol, but one of the guards jumped him before he had a chance to draw it.

Torlos seized the man by one leg and an arm and, tensing his huge muscles, hurled him thirty feet against the Commanding One with such force that both were killed instantly! He turned and grabbed another before his first victim had landed and hurled him toward the advancing guards. Arcot thought fleetingly that here was proof of Torlos' story of being from Nansal; the greater gravity of the third planet made him a great deal stronger than the Satorians!

One of the guards was trying to reach for Arcot. Acting instinctively, the Earthman lashed out with a hard jab to the point of the Satorian's jaw. The iron bones transmitted the shock beautifully to the delicate brain; the man's head jerked back, and he collapsed to the floor. Arcot's hand felt as though he'd hit it with a hammer, but he was far too busy to pay any attention to the pain.

Morey, too, had realized the futility of trying to overcome the guards by wrestling. The only thing to do was dodge and punch. The guards were trying to take the Earthmen alive, but, because of their greater weight, they couldn't move quite as fast as Arcot and Morey.

Torlos was still in action. He had seen the success of the Earthmen who, weak as they were, had been able to knock a man out with a blow to the jaw. Driving his own fists like pistons, he imitated their blows with deadly results; every man he struck went down forever.

The dead were piling around him, but through the open door he could see reinforcements arriving. Somehow, he had to save these Earthmen; if Sator got their secrets, Nansal would be lost!

He reached down and grabbed one of the fallen men and hurled him across the room, smashing back the men who struggled to attack. Then he picked up another and followed through with a second projectile. Then a third. With the speed and tirelessness of some giant engine of war, he slammed his macabre ammunition against the oncoming reinforcements with telling results.

At last Arcot was free for a moment, and that was all he needed. He jerked his molecular ray pistol from its holster and beamed it mercilessly toward the door, hurling the attackers violently backwards. They died instantly, their chilled corpses driving back against their comrades with killing force.

In a moment, every man in the room was dead except for the two Earthmen and the giant Torlos.

Outside the room, they could hear shouted orders as more of the Satorian guards were rallied.

"They'll try to kill us now!" Arcot said. "Come on, we've got to get out of here!"

"Sure," said Morey, "but which way?"

XVII

"Morey, pull down the wall over that door to block their passage," Arcot ordered. "I'll get the other wall."

Arcot pointed his pistol and triggered it. The outer wall flew outward in an explosion of flying masonry. He switched on his radio and called the *Ancient Mariner*.

"Wade! We were cut off because of the metal in the walls! We've been doublecrossed—they tried to jump us. Torlos warned us in time. We've torn out the wall; just hang outside with the airlock open and wait for us. Don't use the rays, because we'll be invisible, and you might hit us."

Suddenly the room rocked under an explosion, and the debris Morey's ray had torn down over the door was blasted away. A score of men leaped through the gap before the dust had settled. Morey beamed them down mercilessly before they could fire their weapons.

"In the air, quick!" Arcot yelled. He turned on his power suit and rose into the air, signalling Torlos to grab his ankles as he had done before. Morey slammed another parting shot toward the doorway as he lifted himself toward the ceiling. Then both Earthmen snapped on their invisibility units. Torlos, because of his direct contact with Arcot, also vanished from sight.

More of the courageous, but foolhardy Satorians leaped through the opening and stared in bewilderment as they saw no one moving. Arcot, Morey, and Torlos were hanging invisible in the air above them.

Just then, the shining bulk of the *Ancient Mariner* drifted into view. They drew back behind the wall and sought shelter. One of them began to fire his compressed air gun at it with absolutely no effect; the heavy lux walls might as well have been hit by a mosquito.

As the airlock swung open, Arcot and Morey headed out through the breach in the wall. A moment later, they were inside the ship. The heavy door hissed closed behind them as they settled to the floor.

"I'll take the controls," Arcot said. "Morey, head for the rear; you take the moleculars and take Torlos with you to handle the heat beam." He turned and ran toward the control room, where Wade and Fuller were waiting. "Wade, take the forward molecular beams; Fuller, you handle the heat projector."

Arcot strapped himself into the control chair.

Suddenly, there was a terrific explosion, and the titanic mass of the ship was rocked by the detonation of a bomb one of the men in the building had fired at the ship.

Torlos had evidently understood the operation of the heat beam projector quickly; the stabbing beam reached out, and the great tower, from floor to roof, suddenly leaned over and slumped as the entire side of the building was converted into a mass of glowing stone and molten steel. Then it crashed heavily to the ground a half mile below.

But already there were forty of the great battleships rising to meet them.

140

"I think we'd better get moving," Arcot said. "We can't let a magnetic ray touch us now; it would kill Torlos. I'm going to cut in the invisibility units, so don't use the heat beams whatever you do!"

Arcot snapped the ship into invisibility and darted to one side. The enemy ships suddenly halted in their wild rush and looked around in amazement for their opponent.

Arcot was heading for the magnetic force field which surrounded the city when Torlos made a mistake. He turned the powerful heat beam downwards and picked off an enemy battleship. It fell, a blazing wreck, but the ray touched a building behind it, and the ionized air established a conducting path between the ship and the planet.

The apparatus was not designed to make a planet invisible, but it made a noble effort. As a result one of the tubes blew, and the *Ancient Mariner* was visible again. Arcot had no time to replace the tube; the Satorian fleet kept him too busy.

Arcot drove the ship, shooting, twisting upward; Wade and Morey kept firing the molecular beams with precision. The pale rays reached out to touch the battleship, and wherever they touched, the ships went down in wreckage, falling to the city below. In spite of the odds against it, the *Ancient Mariner* was giving a good account of itself.

And always, Arcot was working the ship toward the magnetic wall and the base of the city.

Suddenly, giant pneumatic guns from below joined in the battle, hurling huge explosive shells toward the Earthship. They managed to hit the *Ancient Mariner* twice, and each time the ship was staggered by the force of the blast, but the foot-thick armor of lux metal ignored the explosions.

The magnetic rays touched them a few times, and each time Torlos was thrown violently to the floor, but the ship was in the path of the beams for so short a time that he was not badly injured. He more than made up for his injuries with the ray he used, and Morey was no mean gunner, either, judging from the work he was doing.

Three ships attempted to commit suicide in their efforts

to destroy the Earthmen. They were only semi-successful; they managed to commit suicide. In trying to crash into the ship, they were simply caught by Morey's or Wade's molecular beam and thrown away. Morey actually developed a use for them. He caught them in the beam and used them as bullets to smash the other ships, throwing them about on the molecular ray until they were too cold to move.

Arcot finally managed to reach the magnetic wall.

"Wade!" he called. "Get that projector building!"

A molecular beam reached down, and the black metal dome sailed high into the sky, breaking the solidity of the magnetic wall. An instant later, the *Ancient Mariner* shot through the gap. In a few moments, they would be far away from the city.

Torlos seemed to realize this. Moving quickly, he pushed Morey away from the molecular beam projector, taking the controls away from him.

He did not realize the power of that ray; he did not know that these projectors could move whole suns out of their orbits. He only knew that they were destructive. They were several miles from the city when he turned the projector on it, after twisting the power control up.

To his amazement, he saw the entire city suddenly leap into the air and flash out into space, a howling meteor that vanished into the cloudbank overhead. Behind it was a deep hole in the planet's surface, a might chasm lined with dark granite.

Torlos stared at it in amazement and horror.

Arcot turned back slowly, and they sailed over the spot where the city had been. They saw a dozen or so battleships racing away from them to spread the news of the disaster; they were the few which had been fortunate enough to be outside the city when the beam struck.

Arcot maneuvered the ship directly over the mighty pit and sank slowly down, using the great searchlights to illuminate the dark chasm. Far, far down, he could see the solid rock of the bottom. The thing was miles deep.

Then Arcot lifted the ship and headed up through the

cloud layer and into the bright light of the great yellow sun, above the sea of gray misty clouds.

Arcot signalled Morey, who had come into the control room, to take over the controls of the ship. "Head out into space, Morey. I want to find out why Torlos pulled that last stunt. Wade, will you put a new tube in the invisibility unit?"

"Sure," Wade replied. "By the way, what happened back there? We were surprised as the very devil to hear you yelling for help; everything seemed peaceful up to then."

Arcot flexed his bruised hands and grinned ruefully. "Plenty happened." He went on to explain to Wade and Fuller what had happened in their meeting with the Satorian Commander.

"Nice bunch of people to deal with," Wade said caustically. "They tried to get everything and lost it all. We would have given them plenty if they'd been decent about it. But what sort of war is this that the people of these two planets are carrying on, anyway?"

"That's the question I intend to settle," replied Arcot. "We haven't had an opporutnity to talk to Torlos yet. He had just admitted to me that he was a spy for Nansal when the fun began, and we've been too busy to ask questions ever since. Come on, let's go into the library."

Arcot indicated to Torlos that he was to go with him. Wade and Fuller followed.

When they had all seated themselves, Arcot began the telepathic questioning. "Torlos, why did you force Morey to leave the ray and then destroy the city? You certainly had no reason to kill all the non-combatant women and children in that city, did you? And why, after I told you absolutely not to use the heat beam while we were invisible, did you use the rays on that battleship? You made our invisibility break down and destroyed a tube. Why did you do this?"

"I am sorry, man of Earth," replied Torlos. "I can only say that I did not fully understand the effect the rays would have. I did not know how long we would remain invisible; the thing has been accomplished in our laboratories, but only for fractions of a second, and I feared we might become visible soon. That was one of their latest battleships, equipped with a new, secret, and very deadly weapon. I do not know exactly what the weapon is, but I knew that ship could be deadly against us, and I wanted to make sure we were not attacked by it. That is why I used the beam while your ship was invisible.

"And I did not intend to destroy the city. I was only trying to tear up the factory that builds these battleships; I only wanted to destroy their machines. I had no conception of the power of that ray. I was as horrified to see the city disappear as you were; I only wanted to protect my people." Torlos smiled bitterly. "I have lived among these treacherous people for many years, and I cannot say that I had no provocation to destroy their city and everyone in it. But I had no intention of doing it, Earthman."

Arcot knew he was sincere. There could be no deception when communicating telepathically. He wished he had used it when communicating with the Commanding One of Sator; the trouble would have been stopped quickly!

"You still do not have any conception of the magnitude of the power of that beam, Torlos," Arcot told him. "With the rays of this ship, we tore a sun from its orbit and threw it into another. What you did to that city, we could do to the whole planet. Do not tamper with forces you do not understand, Torlos.

"There are forces on this ship that would make the energies of your greatest battleship seem weak and futile. We can race through space a billion times faster than the speed of light; we can tear apart and destroy the atoms of matter; we can rip apart the greatest of planets; we can turn the hurtling stars and send them where we want them; we can curve space as we please; we can put out the fires of a sun, if we wish.

"Torlos, respect the powers of this ship, and do not release its energies unknowingly; they are too great."

Torlos looked around him in awe. He had seen the engines—small, apparently futile things, compared with the solid might of the giant engines in his ship—but he had seen explosive charges that he knew would split any ship open from end to end bounce harmlessly from the smooth walls of this ship. He had seen it destroy the fleet of magnetic ships that had formed a supposedly impregnable guard around the mightest city of Sator.

Then he himself had touched a button, and the giant city had shot off into space, leaving behind it only a screaming tornado and a vast chasm in the crust of the blasted planet.

He could not appreciate the full significance of the velocities Arcot had told him about—he only knew that he had made a bad mistake in underrating the powers of this ship! "I will not touch these things again without your permission, Earthman," Torlos promised earnestly.

The *Ancient Mariner* drove on through space, rapidly eating up the millions of miles that separated Nansal from Sator. Arcot sat in the control room with Morey discussing their passenger.

"You know," Arcot mused, "I've been thinking about that man's strength; an iron skeleton doesn't explain it all. He has to have muscles to move that skeleton around."

"He's got muscles, all right," Morey grinned. "But I see what you mean; muscles that big should tire easily, and his don't seem to. He seems tireless; I watched him throw those men one after another like bullets from a machine gun. He threw the last one as violently as the first—and those men weighed over three hundred pounds! Apparently his muscles felt no fatigue!"

"There's another thing," pointed out Arcot. "The way he was breathing and the way he seemed to keep so cool. When I got through there, I was dripping with sweat; that hot, moist air was almost too much for me. Our friend? Cool as ever, if not more so.

"And after the fight, he wasn't even breathing heavily!"

"No," agreed Morey. "But did you notice him *during* the fight? He was breathing heavily, deeply, and swiftly—not the shallow, panting breath of a runner, but deep and

145

full, yet faster than I can breathe. I could hear him breathing in spite of all the noise of the battle."

"I noticed it," Arcot said. "He started breathing *before* the fight started. A human being can fight very swiftly, and with tremendous vigor, for ten seconds, putting forth his best effort, and only breathe once or twice. For another two minutes, he breathes more heavily than usual. But after that, he can't just slow down back to normal. He has used up the surplus oxygen in his system, and that has to be replaced; he has run into 'oxygen debt'. He has to keep on breathing hard to get back the oxygen surplus his body requires.

"But not Torlos! No fatigue for him! Why? *Because he doesn't use the oxygen of the air to do work, and therefore his body is not a chemical engine!*"

Morey nodded slowly. "I see what you're driving at. His body uses the heat energy of the air! His muscles turn heat energy into motion the same way our molecular beams do!"

"Exactly—he lives on heat!" Arcot said. "I've noticed that he seems almost cold-blooded; his body is at the temperature of the room at all times. In a sense, he is reptilian, but he's vastly more efficient and greatly different than any reptile Earth ever knew. He eats food, all right, but he only needs it to replace his body cells and to fuel his brain."

"Oh, *brother*," said Morey softly. "No wonder he can do the things he did! Why, he could have kept up that fight for hours without getting tired! Fatigue is as unknown to him as cold weather. He'd only need sleep to replace worn parts. His world is warm and upright on its axis, so there are no seasons. He couldn't survive in the Arctic, but he's obviously the ideal form of life for the tropics."

As the two men found out later, Morey was wrong on that last point. The men of Torlos' race had a small organ, a mass of cells in the lower abdomen which could absorb food from the bloodstream and oxidize it, yielding heat, whenever the temperature of the blood dropped below a certain point. Then they could live very comfortably in the Arctic zones; they carried their own heaters. Their vast strength

146

was limited then, however, and they were forced to eat more and were more subject to fatigue.

Wade and Fuller had been trying to speak with Torlos telepathically, and had evidently run into difficulty, for Fuller called into the control room: "Hey, Arcot, come here a minute! I thought telepathy was a universal language, but this guy doesn't get our ideas at all! And we can't make out some of his. Just now, he seemed to be thinking of 'nourishment' or 'food', and I found out he was thinking of 'heat'!"

"I'll be right down," Arcot told him, heading for the library.

As he entered, Torlos smiled at him; Arcot picked up his thought easily: "Your friends do not seem to understand my thoughts."

"We are not made as you are," Arcot explained, "and our thought forms are different. To you, 'heat' and 'food' are practically the same thing, but we do not think of them as such."

He continued, explaining carefully to Torlos the differences between their bodies and their methods of using energy.

"Stone bones!" Torlos thought in amazement. "And chemical engines for muscles! No wonder you seem so weak. And yet, with your brains, I would hate to have to fight a war with your people!"

"Which brings me to another point," Arcot continued. "We would like to know how the war between the people of Sator and the people of Nansal began. Has it been going on very long?"

Torlos nodded. "I will tell you the story. It is a history that began many centuries ago; a history of persecution and rebellion. And yet, for all that, I think it an interesting history.

"Hundreds of years ago, on Nansal . . ."

XVIII

HUNDREDS OF YEARS AGO, on Nansal, there had lived a wise and brilliant teacher named Norus. He had developed an ideal, a philosophy of life, a code of ethics. He had taught the principles of nobility without arrogance, pride without stubbornness, and humility without servility.

About him had gathered a group of men who began to develop and spread his ideals. As the new philosophy spread across the planet, more and more Nansalians adopted it and began to raise their children according to its tenets.

But no philosophy, however workable, however noble, can hope to convert everyone. There always remains a hard core of men who feel that "the old way is the best way". In this case, it was the men whose lives had been based on cunning, deceit, and treachery.

One of these men, a brilliant, but warped genius, named Sator, had built the first spaceship, and he and his men had fled Nansal to set up their own government and free themselves from the persecution they believed they suffered at the hands of the believers of Norus.

They fled to the second planet, where the ship crashed and the builder, Sator, was killed. For hundreds of years, nothing was heard of the emigrants, and the people of Nansal believed them dead. Nansal was at peace.

But the Satorians managed to live on the alien world, and they built a civilization there, a civilization based on an entirely different system. It was a system of cunning. To them, cunning was right. The man who could plot most cunningly, gain his ends by deceiving his friends best, was the man who most deserved to live. There were a few restrictions; they had loyalty, for one thing—loyalty to their country and their world.

In time, the Satorians rediscovered the space drive, but by this time, living on the new planet had changed them physically. They were somewhat smaller than the Nansalians, and lighter in color, for their world was always sunless. The warm rays of the sun had tanned the skins of the Nansalians to a darker color.

When the Satorians first came to Nansal, it was presumably in peace. After so many hundreds of years without war, the Nansalians accepted them, and trade treaties were signed. For years, the Satorians traded peacefully.

In the meantime, Satorian spies were working to find the strengths and weaknesses of Nansal, searching to discover their secret weapons and processes, if any. And they rigorously guarded their own secrets. They refused to disclose the secrets of the magnetic beam and the magnetic space drive.

Finally, there were a few of the more suspicious Nansalians who realized the danger in such a situation. There were three men, students in one of the great scientific schools of Nansal, who realized that the situation should be studied. There was no law prohibiting the men of Nansal from going to Sator, but it seemed that Nature had raised a more impenetrable barrier.

All Nansalians who went to Sator died of a mysterious disease. A method was found whereby a man's body could be sterilized, bacteriologically speaking, so he could not spread the disease, and this was used on all Satorians entering Nansal. But you can't sterilize a whole planet. Nansalians could not go to Sator.

But these three men had a different idea. They carefully studied the speech and the mannerisms and customs of the Satorians. They learned to imitate the slang and idioms. They went even further; they picked three Satorian spaceship navigators and studied them minutely every time they got a chance, in order to learn their habits and their speech patterns. The three Satorians were exceptionally large men, almost perfect doubles of the three Nansalians—and, one by one, the Nansalians replaced them.

They had bleached their faces, and surgeons, working from photographs, changed their features so that the three Nansalians were exact doubles of the three astrogators. Then they acted. On three trips, one of the men that went back as navigator was a Nansalian.

It was six years before they returned to Nansal, but when they finally did, they had learned two things.

In the first place, the 'disease' which had killed Nansalians who had come in contact with Satorians on Nansal was nothing but a poison which acted on contact with the skin. The Nansalians who had gone to Sator had simply been murdered. There was no disease; it had simply been a Satorian plot to keep Nansalians from going to Sator.

The second thing they had learned was the secret of the Satorian magnetic space drive.

It was common knowledge on Sator that their commander would soon lead them across space to conquer Nansal and settle on a world of clear air and cloudless skies, where they could see the stars of space at night. They were waiting only until they could build up a larger fleet and learned all they could from the Nansalians.

They attacked three years after the three Nansalian spies returned with their information.

During those three years, Nansal had secretly succeeded in building up a fleet of the magnetic ships, but it went down quickly before the vastly greater fleet of the Satorians. Their magnetic rays were deadly, killing everyone they struck. They could lift the iron-boned Nansalians high into the air, then drop them hundreds of feet to their death.

The buildings, with their steel and iron frames, went down, crushing hundreds of others. They practically depopulated the whole planet.

But the warnings of the three spies had been in time.

They had enlarged some of the great natural caverns and dug others out of solid rock. Here they had built laboratories, factories, and dwelling places far underground, where the Satorians could never find them.

Enough men reached the caverns before the disaster struck to carry on. They had been chosen from the strongest, healthiest, and most intelligent that Nansal had. They lived there for over a century, while the planet was overrun by the conquerors and the cities were rebuilt by the Satorians.

During this century, the magnetic ray shield was developed by the hidden Nansalians. Daring at last to face their conquerors, they built a city on the surface and protected it with the magnetic force screen.

By the time the Satorians found the city, it was too late. A battle fleet was mobilized and rushed to the spot, but the city was impregnable. The great domed power stations were already in operation, and they were made of nonmagnetic materials, so they could not be pulled from the ground. The magnetic beams were neutralized by the shield, and no ship could pass through it without killing every man aboard.

That first city was a giant munitions plant. The Nansalians built factories there and laughed while the armies of Sator raged impotently at the magnetic barrier. They tried sending missiles through, but the induction heating in every metal part of the bombs either caused them to explode instantly or to drop harmlessly and burn.

In the meantime, the men of Nansal were building their fleet. The Satorians stepped up production, too, but the Nansalians had developed a method of projecting the magnetic screen. Any approaching Satorian ship had its magnetic support cut from under it, and it crashed to the ground.

It took nearly thirty years of hard work and harder fighting for the Nansalians to convince the people of Sator that Nansal and the philosophy of Norus had not only not been wiped out, but was capable of wiping out the Satorians.

With their screened and protected fleet, the followers of

Norus smashed the Satorian cities, and drove their enemy back to Sator.

There were only three enemy cities left on Nansal when, somehow, they managed to learn the secret of the magnetic screen.

By this time, the forces of Nansal had increased tremendously, and they developed the next surprise for the Satorians. One after another, the three remaining cities were destroyed by a barrage of poison gas.

The fleet of Sator tried to retaliate, but the Nansalians were prepared for them. Every building had been sealed and filters had been built into the air conditioning systems.

Shortly, the men of Nansal were again in control of their planet, and the fleet stood guard over the planet.

The Satorians, beaten technologically, were still not ready to give up. Falling back on their peculiar philosophy of life, they pulled a trick the Nansalians would never have thought of. They sued for peace.

The government of Nansal was willing; they had had enough of bloodshed. They permitted a delegation to arrive. The ship was escorted into the city and the parleying began.

The Satorian delegation asked for absolutely unreasonable terms. They demanded fleet bases on Nansal; they demanded an unreasonable rate of exchange between the two powers, one which would be highly favorable to Sator; they wanted to impose fantastic restrictions on Nansalian travel and none whatsoever on their own.

Month followed month and months became years as the diplomats of Nansal tried, patiently and logically, to show the Satorians how unreasonable their demands were.

Not once did they suspect that the Satorians had no intention of trying to get the conditions they asked for. Their sole purpose was to drag the parelying on and on, bickering, quarreling, demanding, and conceding just enough to give the Nansalians hope that a treaty might eventually be consummated.

And during all that time, the factories of Sator were working furiously to build the greatest fleet that had ever crossed the space between the two planets!

When they were ready to attack, the Satorian delegation told Nansal frankly that they would not treaty with them. The day the delegation left, the Satorian fleet swept down upon Nansal!

The Nansalians were again beaten back into their cities, safe behind their magnetic screens, but unable to attack. But the forces of Sator had not won easily—they had, in fact, not won at all. Their supply line was too long and their fleet had suffered greatly at the hands of the defenders of Nansal.

For a long while, the balance of power was so nearly equal that neither side dared attack.

Then the balance again swung toward Nansal. A Nansalian scientist discovered a compact method of storing power. Oddly enough, it was similar to the method Dr. Richard Arcot had discovered a hundred thousand light centuries away! It did not store nearly the power, and was inefficient, but it was a great improvement over their older method of generating energy in the ship itself.

The Nansalian ships could be made smaller, and lighter, and more maneuverable, and at the same time could be equipped with heavier, more powerful magnetic beam generators.

Very shortly, the Satorians were again at the mercy of Nansal. They could not fight the faster, more powerful ships of the Nansalians, and again they went down in defeat.

And again they sued for peace.

This time, Nansal knew better; they went right on developing their fleet while the diplomats of Sator argued.

But the Satorians weren't fools; they didn't expect Nansal to swallow the same bait a second time. Sator had another ace up her sleeve.

Ten days after they arrived, every diplomat and courier of the Satorian delegation committed suicide!

Puzzled, the government of Nansal reported the deaths

to Sator at once, expecting an immediate renewal of hostilities; they were quite sure that Sator assumed they had been murdered. Nansal was totally unprepared for what happened; Sator acknowledged the message with respects and said they would send a new commission.

Two days later, Nansal realized it had been tricked again. A horrible disease broke out and spread like wildfire. The incubation period was twelve days; during that time it gave no sign. Then the flesh began to rot away, and the victim died within hours. No wonder the ambassadors had committed suicide!

Millions died, including Torlos' own father, during the raging epidemic that followed. But, purely by lucky accident, the Nansalian medical research teams came up with a cure and a preventive inoculation before the disease had spread over the whole planet.

Sator's delegation had inoculated themselves with the disease and, at the sacrifice of their own lives, had spread it on Nansal. Although the Satorians had developed the horribly virulent strain of virus, they had not found a cure; the diplomats knew they were going to die.

Having managed to stop the disease before it swept the planet, the Nansalians decided to pull a trick of their own. Radio communication with Sator was cut off in such a way as to lead the Satorian government to believe that Nansal was dying of the disease.

The scientists of Sator knew that the virus was virulent; in fact, too virulent for its own good. It killed the host every time, and the virus could not live outside a living cell. They knew that shortly after every Nansalian died, the virus, too, would be dead.

Their fleet started for Nansal six months after radio contact had broken off. Expecting to find Nansal a dead planet, they were totally unprepared to find them alive and ready for the attack. The Satorian fleet, vastly surprised to find a living, vigorous enemy, was totally wiped out.

Since that time, both planets had remained in a state of armed truce. Neither had developed any weapon which would enable them to gain an advantage over their enemy. Each was so spy-infested that no move could pass undiscovered.

Stalemate.

XIX

TORLOS SPREAD HIS hands eloquently. "That is the history of our war. Can you wonder that my people were suspicious when your ship appeared? Can you wonder that they drove you away? They were afraid of the men of Sator; when they saw your weapons, they were afraid for their civilization.

"On the other hand, why should the men of Sator fear? They knew that our code of honor would not permit us to make a treacherous attack.

"I regret that my people drove you away, but can you blame them?"

Arcot had to admit that he could not. He turned to Morey. "They were certainly reasonable in driving us from their cities; experience has taught them that it's the safest way. A good offense is always the best defense.

"But experience has taught me that, unlike Torlos, I have to eat. I wonder if it might not be a good idea to get a little rest too—I'm bushed."

"Good idea," agreed Morey. "I'll ask Wade to stand guard while we sleep. If Torlos wants company, he can talk to Wade as well as anyone. I'm due for some sleep myself."

Arcot, Morey, and Fuller went to their rooms for some rest. Arcot and Morey were tired, but after an hour, Fuller rose and went down to the control room where Wade was communicating telepathically with Torlos.

155

"Hello," Wade greeted him. "I thought you were going to join the Snoring Chorus."

"I tried to, but I couldn't get in tune. What have you been doing?"

"I've been talking with Torlos—and with fair success. I'm getting the trick of thought communication," Wade said enthusiastically. "I asked Torlos if he wanted to sleep, and it seems that they do it regularly, one day in ten. And when they sleep, they sleep soundly. It's more of a coma, something like the hibernation of a bear or a possum.

"If you want to do business with Mr. John Doe, and he happens to be asleep, your business will have to wait. It takes something really drastic to wake these people up.

"I remember a remark one of my classmates made while I was going to college. He was totally unconscious of the humor in the thing. He said: 'I've got to go to more lectures. I've been losing a lot of sleep.'

"He intended them to be totally disconnected thoughts, but the rest of us knew his habits, and we almost knocked ourselves out laughing.

"I was just wondering what would happen if a Nansalian were to drop off in class. They'd probably have to call an ambulance or something to carry him home!"

Fuller looked at the giant. "I doubt it. One of his classmates would just tuck him under his arm and take him on home—or to the next lecture. Remember, they only weigh about four hundred pounds on Nansal, which is no more to them than fifty pounds is to us."

"True enough," Wade agreed. "But you know, I'd hate to have him wrap those arms of his about me. He might get excited, or sneeze or something, and—*squish!*"

"You and your morbid imagination." Fuller sat down in one of the seats. "Let's see if we can't get a three-way conversation going; this guy is interesting."

Arcot and Morey awoke nearly three hours later, and the Earthmen ate their breakfast, much to Torlos' surprise.

"I can understand that you need far more food than we do," he commented, "but you only ate a few hours ago. It seems like a tremendous amount of food to me. How could you possibly grow enough in your cities?"

"So *that's* why they don't have any farms!" Fuller said.

"Our food is grown out on the plains outside the cities, where there is room," Arcot explained. "It's difficult, but we have machines to help us. We could never have developed the cone type of city you have, however, for we need huge huge quantities of food. If we were to seal ourselves inside our cities as your people have to protect themselves from enemies, we would starve to death very quickly."

"You know," Morey said, "I'll have to admit that Torlos' people are a higher type of creation than we are. Man, and all other animals on Earth, are parasites of the plant world. We're absolutely incapable of producing our own foods. We can't gather energy for ourselves. We're utterly dependent on plants.

"But these men aren't—at least not so much so. They at least generate their own muscular energy by extracting heat from the air they breathe. They combine all the best features of plants, reptiles, and mammals. I don't know where they'd be classified biologically!"

After the meal, they went to the control room and strapped themselves into the control seats. Arcot checked the fuel gauge.

"We have plenty of lead left," he said to Morey, "and Torlos has assured me that we will be able to get more on Nansal. I suggest we show him how the space control works, so that he can tell the Nansalian scientists about it from personal experience.

"In this sun's gravitational field, we'll lose a lot of power, but as long as it can be replaced, we're all right."

Turning to the Nansalian, Arcot pointed out towards the little spark of light that was Torlos' home planet. "Keep your eyes on that, Torlos. Watch it grow when we use our space control drive."

Arcot pushed the little red switch to the first notch. The air around them pulsed with power for an instant, then space had readjusted itself.

The point that was Nansal grew to a disc, and then it was swiftly leaping toward them, welling up to meet them, expanding its bulk with awesome speed. Torlos watched it tensely.

There was a sudden splintering crash, and Arcot jerked open the circuit in alarm. They were almost motionless again as the stars reeled about them.

Torlos had been nervous. Like any man so effected, he had unconsciously tightened his muscles. His fingers had sunk into the hard plastic of the arm rest on his chair, and crushed it as though it had been put between the jaws of a hydraulic press!

"I'm glad we weren't holding hands," said Wade, eyeing the broken plastic.

"I am very sorry," Torlos thought humbly. "I did not intend to do that. I forgot myself when I saw that planet rushing at me so fast." His chagrin was apparent on his face.

Arcot laughed. "It is nothing, Torlos. We are merely astonished at the terrific strength of your hand. Wade wasn't worried; he was joking!"

Torlos looked relieved, but he looked at the splintered arm rest and then at his hand. "It is best that I keep my too-strong hands away from your instruments."

The ship was falling toward Nansal at a relatively slow rate, less than four miles a second. Arcot accelerated toward the planet for two hours, then began to decelerate. Five hundred miles above the planet's surface, their velocity cut the ship into a descending spiral orbit to allow the atmosphere to check their speed.

The outer lux hull began to heat up, and he closed the relux screens to cut down the radiation from it. When he opened them again, the ship was speeding over the broad plains of the planet.

Torlos told Arcot that by far the greater percentage of the surface of Nansal was land. There was still plenty of water, for their seas were much deeper than those of Earth. Some of the seas were thirty miles deep over broad areas—

hundreds of square miles. As if to compensate, the land surfaces were covered with titanic mountain ranges, some of them over ten miles above sea level.

Torlos, his eyes shining, directed the Earthmen to his home city, the capital of the world-nation.

"Is there no traffic between the cities here, Torlos?" Morey asked. "We haven't seen any ships."

"There's continuous traffic," Torlos replied, "but you have come in far to the north, well away from the regularly scheduled routes. The commerce must be densely populated with warships as well, and both warships and commercial craft are made to look as much alike as possible so that the enemy can not know when ships of war are present and when they are not, and their attacks are more easily beaten off. They are forced to live off our commerce while they are here. Before we invented the magnetic storage device, they were forced to get fuel from our ships in order to make the return journey; they could not carry enough for the round trip."

Suddenly his smile broadened, and he pointed out the forward window. "Our city is behind that next range of mountains!"

They were flying at a height of twenty miles, and the range Torlos indicated was far off in the blue distance, almost below the horizon. As they approached them, the mountains seemed to change slowly as their perspective shifted. They seemed to crawl about on one another like living things, growing larger and changing from blue to blue-green, and then to a rich, verdant emerald.

Soon the ship was rocketing smoothly over them. Ahead and below, in the rocky gorge of the mountains, lay a great cone city, the largest the Earthmen had yet seen. As they approached, they could see another cone behind it—the city was a double cone! They resembled the circus tents of two centuries earlier, connected by a ridge.

"Ah—home!" smiled Torlos. "See—that twin cone idea is new. It was not thus when I left it, years ago. It is growing, growing—and in that new section! See? They have bright

159

colors on all the buildings! And already they are digging foundations out to the left for a third cone!" He was so excited that it was difficult for Arcot to read his thoughts coherently.

"But we won't have to build more fortifications," Torlos continued, "if you will give us the secret of the rays you use!

"But, Arcot, you must hide in the hills now; drop down and deposit me in the hills. I will walk to the city on foot.

"I will be able to identify myself, and I will soon be inside the city, telling the Supreme Three that I have salvation and peace for them!"

"I have a better idea," Arcot told him. "It will save you a long walk. We'll make the ship invisible, and take you close to the city. You can drop, say ten feet from the ship to the ground, and continue from there. Will that be all right?"

Torlos agreed that it would.

Invisible, the *Ancient Mariner* dove down toward the city, stopping only a few hundred feet from the base of the magnetic wall, near one of the gigantic beam stations.

"I will come out in a one-man flier, slowly, and at low altitude, toward that mountain there," Torlos told Arcot, pointing. "Then you may become visible and follow me into the city.

"You need fear no treachery from my people," he assured them. Then, smiling: "As if you need fear treachery from the hands of any people! You have certainly proven your ability to defend yourselves!

"Even if my people were treacherously inclined, they would certainly have been convinced by your escape from the Satorians. And they have undoubtedly heard all about it by now through the secret radios of our spies. After all, I was not the only Nansalian spy there, and some of the others must surely have escaped in the ships that ran away after I destroyed the city." Arcot could feel the sadness in his mind as he thought of the fact that his inadvertent destruction of the city had undoubtedly killed some of his own people.

Torlos paused a moment, then asked: "Is there any message you wish me to give the Supreme Council of Three?"

"Yes," replied Arcot. "Repeat to them the offer we so foolishly made to the Commanding One of Sator. We will give them the molecular ray which tore the city out of the ground, and, as your people have seen, also tore a mountain down. We will give them our heat beam, which will melt anything except the material of which this ship is made. And we will give them the knowledge to make this material, too.

"Best of all, we will give them the secret of the most terrific energy source known to mankind; the energy of matter itself. With these in your hands, Sator will soon be peaceful.

"In return, we ask only two things. They will cost you almost nothing, but they are invaluable to us. We have lost our way. In the vastness of space, we can no longer locate our own galaxy. But our own Island Universe has features which could be distinguished on an astronomical plate, and we have taken photographs of it which your astronomers can compare with their own to help us find our way back.

"In addition, we need more fuel—lead wire. Our space control drive does not use up energy except in the presence of a strong gravitational field; most of it is drained back into our storage coils, with very little loss. But we have used it several times near a large sun, and the power drainage goes up exponentially. We would not have enough to get back home if we happened to run into any more trouble on the way."

Arcot paused a moment, considering. "Those two things are all we really need, but we could like to take back more, if your Council is willing. We would like samples of your books and photographs and other artifacts of your civilization to take back home to our own people.

"That, and peace, are all we ask."

Torlos nodded. "The things you ask, I am sure the Council

161

will readily agree to. It seems little enough payment for the things you intend to do for us."

"Very well, then. We will wait for you. Good luck!"

Torlos turned and jumped out of the airlock. The ship rose high above him as he suddenly became visible on the plain below. He was running toward the city in great leaps of twenty feet—graceful, easy leaps that showed his tremendous power.

Suddenly, a ship was darting down from the city toward him. As it curved down, Torlos stopped and made certain signals with his arms, then he stood quietly with his hands in the air.

The ship hovered above him, and two men dropped thirty feet to the ground and questioned him for several minutes.

Finally, they motioned to the ship, which dropped to ten feet, and the three men leaped lightly to its door and entered. The door snapped shut, and the ship shot toward the city. The magnetic wall opened for a moment, and the ship shot through. Within seconds, it was out of sight, lost in the busy air traffic above the city.

"Well," said Arcot, "now we go back to the hills and wait."

XX

FOR TWO DAYS, the *Ancient Mariner* lay hidden in the hills. It was visible all that time, but at least two of the men were watching the sky every hour of the day. Torlos himself was, they knew, perfectly trustworthy, but they did not know whether his people were as honorable as he claimed them to be.

Arcot and Wade were in the control room on the afternoon of the second day—not Earth days, but the forty-hour Nansalian days—and they had been quietly discussing the biological differences between themselves and the inhabitants of this planet.

Suddenly, Wade saw a slowly moving speck in the sky. "Look, Arcot! There's Torlos!"

They waited, ready for any hostile action as the tiny ship approached rapidly, circling slowly downward as it came nearer. It landed a few hundred feet away, and Torlos emerged, running rapidly toward the Earth ship. Arcot let him in through the airlock.

Torlos smiled broadly. "I had difficulty in convincing the Council that my story was true. When I told them that you could go faster than light, they strongly objected. But they had to admit that you had certainly been able to tear down the mountain very effectively, and they had received reports of the destruction of the Satorian capitol.

"It seems you first visited the city of Thanso when you came here. The people were nearly panic-stricken when they saw you rip that mountain down and uproot the magnetic ray station. No one ship had ever done that before!

"But the fact that several guards had seen me materialize out of thin air, plus the fact that they knew you could make yourselves invisible, convinced them that my story was true.

"They want to talk to you, and they say that they will gladly grant your requests. But you must promise them one thing—you must stay away from any of our people, for they are afraid of disease. Bacteria that do not bother you very much might be deadly to us. The Supreme Council of Three is willing to take the risk, but they will not allow anyone else to be exposed."

"We will keep apart from your people if the Council wishes," Arcot agreed, "but there is no real danger. We are so vastly different from you that it will be impossible for you to get our diseases, or for us to contract yours. However, if the Council wants it, we will do as they ask."

Torlos at once went back to his ship and headed toward the city.

Arcot followed in the *Ancient Mariner,* keeping about three hundred feet to the rear.

When they reached the magnetic screen of the city, one of the beam stations cut its power for a few moments, leaving a gap for the two ships to glide smoothly through.

On the roofs of the buildings, men and women were collected, watching the shining, polished hull of the strange ship as it moved silently above them.

Torlos led them to the great central building and dropped to the huge landing field beside it. All around them, in regular rows, the great hulls of the Nansal battleships were arranged. Arcot landed the *Ancient Mariner* and shut off the power.

"I think Wade is the man to go with me this time," Arcot said. "He has learned to communicate with Torlos quite well. We will each carry both pistols and wear our power suits. And we'll be in radio communicaton with you at all times.

"I don't think they'll start anything we don't like this time, but I'm not as confident as I was, and I'm not going to take any useless chances. This time I'm going to make arrangements. If I die here, there's going to be a very costly funeral, and these men are going to pay the costs!

"I'll call you every three minutes, Morey. If I don't, check up on me. If you still don't get an answer, take this place apart because you won't be able to hurt us then.

"I'm going to tell Torlos about our precautions. If the building shields the radio, I'll be listening for you and I'll retrace my steps until I can contact you again. Right? Then come on, Wade!" Arcot, fully equipped, strode down the corridor to the airlock.

Torlos was waiting for them with another man, whom Torlos explained was a high-ranking officer of the fleet. Torlos, it seemed, was without official rank. He was a secret service agent without official status, and therefore an officer had been assigned to accompany the Earthmen.

ISLANDS OF SPACE

Torlos seemed to be relaxing in the soft, warm sunlight of his native world. It had been years since he had seen that yellow sun except from the windows of a space flier. Now he could walk around in the clear air of the planet of his birth.

Arcot explained to him the precautions they had taken against trouble here, and Torlos smiled. "You have certainly learned greater caution. I can't blame you. We certainly seem little different from the men of Sator; we can only stand on trial. But I know you will be safe."

They walked across the great court, which was covered with a soft, springy turf of green. The hot sun shining down on them, the brilliant colors of the buildings, the towering walls of the magnificent edifice they were approaching, and, behind them, the shining hull of the *Ancient Mariner* set among the dark, needle-shaped Nansalian ships, all combined to make a picture that would remain in their minds for a long time.

Here, there were no guards watching them as they were conducted to the meeting of the Supreme Council of Three.

They went into the main entrance of the towering government building and stepped into the great hall on the ground floor. It was like the interior of an ancient Gothic cathedral, beautiful and dignified. Great pillars of green stone rose in graceful, fluted columns, smoothly curving out like the branches of some stylized tree to meet in arches that rose high in pleasing curves to a point midway between four pillars. The walls were made of a dark green stone as a background; on them had been traced designs in colored tile.

The whole hall was a thing of colored beauty; the color gave it life, as the yellow sunlight gave life to the trees of the mountains.

They crossed the great hall and came at last to the elevator. Its door was made of narrow strips of metal, so bound together that the whole made a flexible, but strong sheet. In principle, the doors worked like the cover of an antique roll-top desk. The idea was old, but these men had made their elevator doors very attractive by the addition of color. In no way did they detract from the dignified grace of the magnificent hall.

Torlos turned to Arcot. "I wonder if it would not be wise to shut off your radio as we enter the elevator. Might not the magnetic force affect it?"

"Probably," Arcot agreed. He contacted Morey and told him that the radio would be cut off for a short while. "But it won't be more than three minutes," Arcot finished. "If it is—you know what to do."

As they entered the elevator, Torlos smiled at the two Earthmen. "We will ascend more gradually this time, so that the acceleration won't be so tiring to you." He moved the controls carefully, and by gentle steps they rose to the sixty-third floor of the giant building.

As they stepped out of the elevator, Torlos pointed toward an open window that stretched widely across one wall. Below them, they could see the *Ancient Mariner*.

"Your radio contact should be good," Torlos commented.

Wade put in a call to Morey, and to his relief, he made contact immediately.

The officer was leading them down a green stone corridor toward a simple door. He opened it, and they entered the room beyond.

In the center of the room was a large triangular table. At a place at the center of each side sat one man on a slightly raised chair, while on each side of him sat a number of other men.

Torlos stopped at the door and saluted. Then he spoke in rapid, liquid syllables to the men sitting at the table, halting once or twice and showing evident embarrassment as he did so.

He paused, and one of the three men in command replied rapidly in a pleasant voice that had none of the harsh command that Arcot had noticed in the voice of the Satorian Commanding One. Arcot liked the voice and the man.

Judging by Earth standards, he was past middle age— whatever that might be on Nansal—with crisp black hair

166

that was bleaching slightly. His face showed the signs of worry that the making of momentous decisions always leaves, but although the face was strong with authority, there was a gentleness that comes with a feeling of kindly power.

Wade was talking rapidly into the radio, describing the scene before them to Morey. He described the great table of dark wood, and the men about it, some in the blue uniform of the military, and some in the loose, soft garments of the civilian. Their colored fabrics, individually in good taste and harmony, were frequently badly out of harmony with the costume of a neighbor, a difficulty accompanying this brightly tinted clothing.

Torlos turned to Arcot. "The Supreme council asks that you be seated at the table, in the places left for you." He paused, then quickly added: "I have told them of your precautions, and they have said: 'A wise man, having been received treacherously once, will not again be trapped.' They approve of your policy of caution.

"The men who sit at the raised portions of the table are the Supreme Three; the others are their advisors who know the details of Science, Business, and War. No one man can know all the branches of human endeavor, and this is but a meeting place of those who know best the individual lines. The Supreme Three are elected from the advisors in case of the death of one of the Three, and they act as co-ordinators for the rest.

"The man of Science is to your left; directly before you is the man of Business, and to your right is the Commander of the Military.

"To whom do you wish to speak first?"

Arcot considered for a moment, then: "I must first tell the Scientist what it is I have, then tell the Commander how he can use it, and finally I will tell the Businessman what will be needed."

Arcot had noticed that the military officers all wore holsters for their pneumatic pistols, but they were conspicuously empty. He was both pleased and embarrassed. What should he do—he, who carried two deadly pistols. He de-

167

cided on the least conspicuous course and left them where they were.

Arcot projected his thoughts at Torlos. "We have come a vast distance across space, from another galaxy. Let your astronomer tell them what distance that represents."

Arcot paused while Torlos put the thoughts into the words of the Nansalian language. A moment later, one of the scientists, a tall, powerfully built man, even for these men of giant strength, rose and spoke to the others. When he was seated, a second rose and spoke also, with an expression of puzzled wonder.

"He says," Torlos translated, "that his science has taught him that a speed such as you say you have made is impossible, but the fact that you are here proves his science wrong.

"He reasoned that since your kind live on no planet of this system, you must come from another star. Since his science says that this is just as impossible as coming from another galaxy, he is convinced of the fallacy in the theories."

Arcot smiled. The sound reasoning was creditable; the man did not label as "impossible" something which was proven by the presence of the two Earthmen.

Arcot tried to explain the physical concepts behind his space-strain drive, but communication broke down rapidly; Torlos, a warrior, not a scientist, could not comprehend the ideas, and was completely unable to translate them into his own language.

"The Chief Physicist suggests that you think directly at him," Torlos finally told Arcot. "He suggests that the thoughts might be more familiar to him than to me." He grinned. "And they certainly aren't clear to me!"

Arcot projected his thoughts directly toward the physicist; to his surprise, the man was a perfect receiver. He had a natural gift for it. Quickly, Arcot outlined the system that had made his intergalactic voyage possible.

The physicist smiled when Arcot was finished, and tried to reply, but he was not a good transmitter. Torlos aided him.

"He says that the science of your people is far ahead of us. The conceptions are totally foreign to his mind, and he can only barely grasp the significance of the idea of bent emptiness that you have given him. He says, however, that he can fully appreciate the possibility that you have shown him. He has given your message to the Three, and they are anxious to hear of the weapons you have."

Arcot drew the molecular pistol, and holding it up for all to see, projected the general theory of its operation toward the physicist.

To the Chief Physicist of Nansal, the idea of molecular energy was an old one; he had been making use of it all his life, and it was well known that the muscles used the heat of air to do their work. He understood well how it worked, but not until Arcot projected into his mind the mental impression of how the Earthmen had thrown one sun into another did he realize the vast power of the ray.

Awed, the man translated the idea to his fellows.

Then Arcot drew the heat pistol and explained how the annihilation of matter within it was converted into pure heat by the relux lens.

"I will show you how they work," Arcot continued. "Could we have a lump of metal of some kind?"

The Scientist spoke into an intercom microphone, and within a few minutes, a large lump of iron—a broken casting—was brought in. Arcot suspended it on the molecular beam while Wade melted it with the heat beam. It melted and collapsed into a ball that glowed brilliantly and flamed as its surface burned in the oxygen of the air. Wade cut off his heat ray, and the ball quickly cooled under the influence of the molecular beam until Arcot lowered it to the floor, a perfect sphere crusted with ice and frost.

Arcot continued for the better part of an hour to explain to the Council exactly what he had, how they could be used, and what materials and processes were needed to make them.

When he was finished, the Supreme Three conferred for several minutes. Then the Scientist asked, through Torlos:

"How can we repay you for these things you have given us?"

"First, we need lead to fuel our ship." Arcot gave them the exact specifications for the lead wire they needed.

He received his answer from the man of Business and Manufacturing. "We can give you that easily, for lead is cheap. Indeed, it seems hardly enough to repay you."

"The second thing we need," Arcot continued, "is information. We became lost in space and are unable to find our way home. I would like to explain the case to the Astronomer."

The Astronomer proved to be a man of powerful intelligence as well as powerful physique, and was a better transmitter than receiver. It took every bit of Arcot's powerful mind to project his thoughts to the man.

He explained the dilemma that he and his friends were in, and told him how he could recognize the Galaxy on his plates. The Astronomer said he thought he knew of such a nebula, but he would like to compare his own photographs with Arcot's to make sure.

"In return," Arcot told him, "we will give you another weapon—a weapon, this time, to defeat the astronomer's greatest enemy, distance. It is an electrical telescope which will permit you to see life on every planet of this system. With it, you can see a man at a distance ten times as great as the distance from Nansal to your sun!"

Eagerly, the Astronomer questioned Arcot concerning the telectroscope, but others were clamoring for Arcot's attention.

The Biologist was foremost among the contenders; he seemed worried about the possibility of the alien Earthmen carrying pathogenic bacteria.

"Torlos has told us that you have an entirely different internal organization. What is it that is different? I can't believe that he has correctly understood you."

Arcot explained the differences as carefully as possible. By the time he was finished, the Biologist felt sure that any such creature was sufficiently far removed from them to be harmless biologically, but he wanted to study the Man of Earth further.

Arcot had brought along a collection of medical books as a possible aid in case of accident. He offered to give these to Nansal in exchange for a collection of Nansalian medical texts. The English would have to be worked out with the aid of a dictionary and a primary working aid which Arcot would supply. Arcot also asked for a skeleton to take with him, and the Biologist readily agreed.

"We'd like to give you one in return," Arcot grinned, "But we only brought four along, and, unfortunately, we are using them at the moment."

The Biologist smiled back and assured him that they would not think of taking a piece of apparatus so vitally necessary to the Earthmen.

The Military Leader was the man who demanded attention next. Arcot had a long conference with him, and they decided that the best way for the Military Leader to learn the war potential of the *Ancient Mariner* was to personally see a demonstration of its powers.

The Council decided that the Three would go on the trip. The Military Commander picked two of his aides to go, and the Scientist picked the Astronomer and the Physicist. The head of Business and Manufacturing declined to bring any of his advisors.

"We would learn nothing," he told Arcot, "and would only be in the way. I, myself, am going only because I am one of the Three."

"Very well," said Arcot. "Let's get started."

XXI

THE PARTY DESCENDED to the ground floor and walked out to the ship. They filed into the airlock, and in the power room they looked in amazement at the tiny machines that ran the ship. The long black cylinder of the main power unit for the molecular drive looked weak and futile compared to the bulky machines that ran their own ships. The power storage coils, with their fields of intense, dead blackness, interested the Physicist immensely.

The ship was a constant source of wonder to them all. They investigated the laboratory and then went up to the second floor. Morey and Fuller greeted them at the door, and each of the four Earthmen took a group around the ship, explaining as they went.

The library was a point of great interest, exceeded only by the control room. Arcot found some difficulty in taking care of all his visitors; there were only four chairs in the control room. The Three could sit down, but Arcot needed the fourth chair to pilot the ship. The rest of the party had to hold on as best they could, which was not too difficult for men of such physical strength; they were accustomed to high accelerations in their elevators.

Morey, Wade, and Fuller strapped themselves into the seats at the ray projectors at the sides and stern.

Arcot wanted to demonstrate the effectiveness of the ship's armament first, and then the maneuverability. He picked a barren hillside for the first demonstration. It was a great rocky cliff, high above the timber line, towering almost vertically a thousand feet above them.

172

Wade triggered his molecular projector, and a pale beam reached out toward the cliff. Instantly, the cliff leaped ten miles into the air, whining and roaring as it shot up through the atmosphere. Then it started to fall. Heated by its motion through the air, it struck the mountaintop as a mass of red hot rock which shattered into fragments with a terrific roar! The rocks rolled and bounced down the mountainside, their path traced by a line of steam clouds.

Then, at Arcot's order, the heat beams were all turned on the mountain at full power. In less than a minute, the peak began to melt, sending streamers of lava down the sides. The beams began to eat out a crater in the center, where the rock began to boil furiously under the terrific energy of the heat beams.

Then Arcot shut off the heat beams and turned on the molecular ray.

The molecules of the molten rock were traveling at high velocities—the heat was terrific. Arcot could see that the rock was boiling quite freely. When the molecular beam hit it, every one of those fast moving molecules shot upward together! With the roar of a meteor, it plunged toward space at five miles a second!

It had dropped to absolute zero when the beam hit it, but at that speed through the air, it didn't stay cold long! Arcot followed it up in the *Ancient Mariner*. It was going too slowly for him. The air had slowed it down and heated it up, so Arcot hit it with the molecular ray again, converting the heat back into velocity.

By the time they reached free space, Arcot had maneuvered the lump of rock into an orbit around the planet.

"Tharlano," he thought at the Astonomer, "your planet now has a new satellite!"

"So I perceive!" replied Tharlano. "Now that we are in space, can we use the instrument you told me of?"

Arcot established the ship in an orbit twenty thousand miles from the planet and led them back to the observatory, where Morey had already trained the telectroscope on the planet below. There wasn't much to see; the amplification showed only the rushing ground moving by so fast that the image blurred.

He turned it to Sator. It filled the screen as they increased the power, but all they could see was billowing clouds. Another poor subject.

Morey showed Tharlano, the Astronomer, how to use the controls, and he began to sweep the sky with the instrument, greatly pleased with its resolving ability and tremendous magnification.

The Military Leader of the Three pointed out that the Satorians still had a weapon that was reported deadly, and they were in imminent danger unless Arcot's inventions were applied at once. All the way back to Nansal, they spent the time discussing the problem in the *Ancient Mariner*'s Library.

It was finally agreed that the necessary plans and blueprints were to be given to the Nansalians, who could start production at once. The biggest problem was in the supply of lux and relux, which, because of their vast energy-content, required the atomic converters of the *Ancient Mariner* to make them. The Earthmen agreed to supply the power and the necessary materials to begin operations.

When the ship landed, a meeting of the manufacturers was called. Fuller distributed prints of the microfilmed plans for the equipment that he had packed in the library, and the factory engineers worked from them to build the necessary equipment.

The days that followed were busy days for Earthmen and Nansalians alike.

The Nansalians were fearful of the consequences of the weapon that the Satorians were rumored to have. The results of their investigations through their agents had, so far, resulted only in the death of the secret service men. All that was known was exactly what the Satorians wanted them to know; the instrument was new, and it was deadly.

On the other hand, the Satorians were not entirely in the dark as to the progress of Nansal, as Arcot and Morey discovered one day.

After months of work designing and tooling up the Nansalian factories, making the tools to make the tools to make the war material needed, and training the engineers of Nansal all over the planet to produce the equipment needed, Arcot and Morey finally found time to take a few days off.

Tharlano had begun a systematic search of the known nebulae, comparing them with the photographs the Earthmen had given him, and looking for a galaxy with two satellite star clouds of exactly the right size and distance from the great spiral.

After months of work, he had finally picked one which filled the bill exactly! He invited Arcot and Morey to the observatory to confirm his findings.

The observatory was located on the barren peak of a great mountain more than nine miles high. It was almost the perfect place for an astronomical telescope. Here, well above the troposphere, the air was thin and always clear. The solid rock of the mountain was far from disturbing influences which might cause any vibration in the telescope.

The observatory was accessible only from a spaceship or air flyer, and, at that altitude, had to be pressurized and sealed against the thin, cold air outside. Within, the temperature was kept constant to a fraction of a degree to keep thermal expansion from throwing the mirror out of true.

Arcot and Morey, accompanied by Tharlano and Torlos, settled the *Ancient Mariner* to the landing field that had been blasted out of the rock of the towering mountain. They went over to the observatory and were at once admitted to the airlock.

The floor was of smoothed, solid rock, and in this, the great clock which timed and moved the telescope was set.

The entire observatory was, of course, surrounded by a magnetic shield, and it was necessary to make sure there were no enemy ships around before using the telescope, because the magnetic field affected the light rays passing through it.

The mirror for the huge reflecting telescope was nearly

175

three hundred inches in diameter, and was powerful enough to spot a spaceship leaving Sator. Its military usefulness, however, was practically nil, since painting the ships black made them totally invisible.

There were half a dozen assistants with Tharlano at the observatory at all times, one of them in charge of the great file of plates that were kept on hand. Every plate made was printed in triplicate, to prevent their being destroyed in a raid. The original was kept at the observatory, and copies were sent to two of the largest cities on Nansal. It was from this file that Tharlano had gathered the data necessary to show Arcot his own galaxy.

Tharlano was proudly explaining the telescope to Arcot, realizing that the telectroscope was far better, but knowing that the Earthmen would appreciate this triumph of mechanical perfection. Arcot and Morey were both intensely interested in the discussion, while Torlos, slightly bored by a subject he knew next to nothing about, was examining the rest of the observatory.

Suddenly, he cried out in warning, and leaped a full thirty feet over the rock floor to gather Arcot and Morey in his great arms. There was a sharp, distinct snap of a pneumatic pistol, and the thud of a bullet. Arcot and Morey each felt Torlos jerk!

Quick as a flash, Torlos pushed the two men behind the great tube of the telescope. He leaped over it and across the room, and disappeared into the supply room. There was the noise of a scuffle, another crack from a pneumatic pistol, and the sudden crash and tinkle of broken glass.

Suddenly, the figure of a man described a wide arc as it flew out of the supply room and landed with a heavy crash on the floor. Instantly, Torlos leaped at him. There was a trickle of blood from his left shoulder, but he gripped the man in his giant arms, pinning him to the floor. The struggle was brief. Torlos simply squeezed the man's chest in his arms. There was the faint creak of metal, and the man's chest began to bend! In a moment, he was unconscious.

Torlos pulled a heavy leather belt off of the unconscious

man and tied his arms with it, wrapping it many times around the wrists, and was picking the man up when Tharlano arrived, followed by Arcot and Morey. Torlos smiled broadly.

"This is one Satorian spy that won't report. I could have finished him when I got my hold on him, but I wanted to take him before the Council for questioning. He'll be all right; I just dented his chest a little."

"We owe our lives to you again, Torlos," Arcot told him gravely. "But you certainly risked your life; the bullet might well have penetrated your heart instead of striking a rib, as it seems to have done."

"Rib? What is a rib?" The thought concept seemed totally unfamiliar to Torlos.

Arcot looked at him oddly, then reached out and ran an exploratory hand over Torlos' chest. It was smooth and solid!

"Morey!" Arcot exclaimed. "These men have no ribs! Their chest is as solid as their skulls!"

"Then how do they breathe?" Morey asked.

"How do you breathe? I mean most of the time. You use your diaphragm and your abdominal muscles. These people do, too!"

Morey grinned. "No wonder Torlos jumped in front of that bullet! He didn't have as much to fear as we do—he had a built-in bullet proof vest! You'd have to shoot him in the abdomen to reach any vital organ."

Arcot turned back to Torlos. "Who is this man?"

"Undoubtedly a Satorian spy sent to murder you Earthmen. I saw the muzzle of his pistol as he was aiming and jumped in the way of the bullet. There is not much damage done."

"We'd better get back to the city," Arcot said. "Fuller and Wade might be in danger!"

They bundled the Satorian spy into the ship, where Morey tied him further with thin strands of lux cable no bigger than a piece of string.

Torlos looked at it and shook his head. "He will break that as soon as he awakens, without even knowing it. You forget the strength of our people."

177

Morey smiled and wrapped the cord around Torlos' wrists.

Torlos looked amused and pulled. His smile vanished. He pulled harder. His huge muscles bulged and writhed in great ridges along his arms. The thin cord remained complacently undamaged. Torlos relaxed and grinned sheepishly.

"You win," he thought. "I'll make no more comments on the things I see you do."

They returned to the capitol at once. Arcot shoved the speed up as high as he dared, for Torlos felt there might be some significance in the attempt to remove Arcot and Morey. Wade and Fuller had already been warned by radio, and had immediately retired to the Council Room of the Three. The members of the Investigation Board joined them to question the prisoner upon his arrival.

When they arrived, Arcot and Morey went in with Torlos, who was carrying the struggling, shackled spy over his shoulder.

The Earthmen watched while the expert interrogators of the Investigation Board questioned the prisoner. The philosophy of Norus did not permit torture, even for a vicious enemy, but the questioners were shrewd and ingenious in their methods. For hours, they took turns pounding questions at the prisoner, cajoling, threatening, and arguing.

They got nowhere. Solidly, the prisoner stuck by his guns. Why had he tried to shoot the Earthmen? He didn't know. What were his orders from Sator? Silence. What were Sator's plans? Silence. Did he know anything of the new weapon? A shrug of the shoulders.

Finally, Arcot spoke to the Chief Investigation Officer. "May I try my luck? I think I'm powerful enough to use a little combination of hypnosis and telepathy that will get the information out of him." The Investigator agreed to try it.

Arcot walked over as if to inspect the prisoner. For an instant, the man looked defiantly at Arcot. Arcot glared back. At the same time, his powerful mind reached out and began to work subtly within the prisoner's brain. Slowly, a

178

helpless, blank expression came over the man's face as his eyes remained fixed on Arcot's own. The man was as help-lessly bound mentally as the lux cable bound him physical-ly.

For a full quarter of an hour, the two men, Earthmen and Satorian, stood locked in a frozen tableau, staring into each other's eyes. The onlookers waited in watchful silence.

Finally, Arcot turned and shook his head, as if to clear it. As he did so, the spy slumped forward in his chair, un-conscious.

Arcot rubbed his own temples and spoke in English to Morey. "Some job! You'll have to tell them what I found out; my head is splitting! With a headache like this, I can't communicate.

"Torlos was right; they were trying to get rid of all four of us. We're the only ones who can operate the ship, and that ship is the only defense against them.

"He knows several other spies here in the city, and we can, I think, practically wipe out the Satorian spy system all over the planet with the information he gave me and what we can get from others we arrest.

"Unfortunately, he doesn't know anything about the new weapon; the higher-ups aren't telling anyone, not even their own men. I get the idea that only those on board the ships using it will know about it before the attack.

"An attack is planned, and very soon. He didn't know when. We can only lie in readiness and do everything we can to help these people with their work."

While Morey relayed this information to the Investigating Board and the Council, Wade was talking in low tones to Arcot.

"They had a lot of workmen bring twenty tons of lead wire on board this evening, and the distilled water tanks are full. The tanks are full of oxygen, and they gave us some synthetic food which we can eat.

"They have it all over us in the field of chemistry. They've found the secret of catalysis, and can actually syn-thesize any catalytic agent they want. They can make any possible reaction go in either direction at any rate they desire.

"They took a slice of flesh from my arm and analyzed it down to the last detail. From that, they were able to predict what sort of food we would need to eat. They can actually synthesize living things!

"I've tried the food they made, and it has a very good flavor. They guaranteed it would have all the necessary ingredients, right down to the smallest trace element!

"We're fully stocked for a long trip. The Three said it was their first consideration that we should be able to return to our homes."

"How about their armament?" Arcot asked. He was holding his head in his hands to ease the throbbing ache within it.

"Each city has a projector supplied by the regular power station on top of their central building. The molecular ray, of course; they still don't have enough power to run a heat beam.

"We didn't have time to make more than one for each city, but this one will give the Satorians a nasty time if they come near it. It works nicely through the magnetic screen, so it won't be necessary for them to lower the barrier to shoot."

Morey had finished telling the Council what Arcot had discovered from the prisoner, and the Councilmen were leaving one by one to go to their duties in preparing for the attack.

"I think we had best go back to the *Ancient Mariner*," Arcot said. "I need an aspirin and some sleep."

"Same here," agreed Fuller. "These men make me feel as though I were lazy. They work for forty or fifty hours and think nothing of it. Then they snooze for five hours and they're ready for another long stretch. I feel like a lounge lizard if I take six hours out of every twenty-four."

They asked Torlos to stand guard on the ship while they got some much needed sleep, and Torlos consented readily after getting the permission of the Supreme Three.

The Earthmen were returned to their ship under heavy guard to prevent further attempts at assassination.

It was seven hours after they had gone to sleep that it came.

Through the ship came the low hum that rose quickly to a screeching call of danger—the warning! The city was under attack!

XXII

THE NANSALIAN FLEET was already outside the city and hard at it. The fight was on! But Arcot saw that the fight was one-sided in the extreme. Ship after ship of the Nansalian fleet seemed to burst into sudden, inexplicable flame and fall blazing against another of their own ships! It seemed as though some irresistible attraction drew the ships together and smashed them against each other in a blaze of electric flame, while the ships of Sator did nothing but stay far off to one side and dodge the rays of the Nansalian ships.

Quickly, Arcot turned to Torlos. "Torlos, go out! Leave the ship! We can work better when you aren't here, since we don't have to worry about exposure to magnetic rays. I don't like to make you miss this, but it's for your world!"

Torlos showed his disappointment; he wanted to be in this battle. But he realized that what the Earthman said was true. Their weak, stone bones were completely immune to the effects of even the most powerful magnetic ray.

He nodded. "I'll go. Good Luck! And give them a few shots for me!"

He turned and ran down the corridor to the airlock. As soon as he was outside, Arcot lifted the ship.

It had taken less than a minute to get into the air, but

in that minute, the Nansalian fleet had taken a terrific beating. Arcot noticed that the few ships of Sator that had been hit smashed into the ground with a terrible blaze of violet light that left nothing but a pile of fused metal.

"They've got something, all right," Arcot thought to himself as he drove the *Ancient Mariner* into battle.

It would be impossible for the Nansalians to lower their magnetic screen, even for a second, so Arcot simply aimed the ship toward it and turned on the power.

"Hold on!" he called as they struck it. The ship reeled and sank suddenly planetward, then it bounced up and outward. They were through the wall.

The rooms were suddenly oppressively hot, and the molecular cooler was struggling to lower it. "We made it," Morey said triumphantly, "but the eddy currents sure heated up the hull!"

They were out of the city now, speeding toward the battle. Following a prearranged system, the Nansalian ships retreated, leaving the Earthmen a free hand. They needed no help!

Wade, Fuller, and Morey began to lash out with the molecular beams, smashing the Satorian ships in on themselves, crushing them to the ground, where they exploded in violet flame.

Wade and Fuller began to work together. Wade caught one ship in the molecular ray, and Fuller hit with a heat beam. Like some titanic broom they swept it around at dozens of miles a second, leaping, twisting, smashing ship after ship. Like a snowball, the lump of glowing metal grew with each crash, till a dozen ships had fallen into it. It was a new broom, and it swept clean!

Then a magnetic beam caught the *Ancient Mariner*. With a shock, it slowed down at a terrific rate. Then Arcot turned on more power, and simply dragged the other ship along by its own magnetic beam! Wade tore the ship loose with his molecular beam, but the mighty mass of metal that had been his broom was gone, a glowing mass of metal on the ground.

"We haven't seen that new weapon yet," Morey called.

"Can't find us!" Arcot replied into the intercom. The sun was setting, and the blazing red star was lighting the ship, making it seem like a ball of fire when still and a flashing streak of red light when in motion.

Ship after ship of the Satorians was going down before the three beams of the Earth ship; the great fleet was dissolving like a lump of sugar in boiling water.

Suddenly, just ahead of them, an enemy ship drove toward them with obvious intent to ram; if his magnetic beam caught them, and drew them towards him, there would be a head-on collision.

Wade caught it with a molecular beam, and it became a blazing wreck on the ground.

"All rays off!" Arcot called. As soon as they were off, Arcot hit a switch, and the *Ancient Mariner* vanished.

Arcot drove the invisible ship high above the battle. Below, the Satorians were searching wildly for the ship. They knew it must be somewhere near, and feared that at any second it might materialize before them with its deadly rays.

Arcot stayed above them for nearly a minute while the ships below twisted and turned, wildly seeking him. Then they went into formation again and started back for the city.

"That's what I wanted!" Arcot said grimly. "In formation, they're like sitting ducks!" He dropped the ship like a plummet while the ray operators prepared to sweep the formation with their beams.

Suddenly the *Ancient Mariner* was visible again. Simultaneously, three rays leaped down and bathed the formation in their pale radiance. The front ranks vanished, and the line broke, attacking the ship that hung above them now. Four magnetic beams hit the *Ancient Mariner* at once! Arcot couldn't pull away from all four, and his gunners couldn't tell which ships were holding them.

All at once, the men felt a violent electrical shock! The air about them was filled with the blue haze of the electric weapon they had seen!

183

Instantly, the magnetic beams left them, and they saw behind them a single Satorian ship heading toward them, surrounded by that same bluish halo of light. A suicide ship!

Arcot accelerated away from it as Fuller hit it with a molecular beam. The ship reeled and stopped, and the *Ancient Mariner* pulled away from it rapidly. Then, the frost-covered ship of the dead came on, still heading for them!

Arcot turned and went off to the right, but like a pursuing Nemesis, the strange ship came after them in the shortest, most direct route!

The molecular beams were useless now; there was no molecular energy left in the frozen hulk that accelerated toward them. Suddenly, the two envelopes of blue light touched and coalesced! A great, blinding arc leaped between the two ships as the speeding Satorian hull smashed violently against the side of the *Ancient Mariner!* The men ducked automatically, and were hurled against their seat-straps with tremendous force. There was a rending, crashing roar, a sea of flame—and darkness.

They could only have been unconscious a few seconds, for when the fog went away, they could see the glowing mass of the enemy ship still falling far beneath them. The lux wall where it had hit was still glowing red.

"Morey!" Arcot called. "You all right? Wade? Fuller?"

"Okay!" Morey answered.

So were Wade and Fuller.

"It was the lux hull that saved us," Arcot said. "It wouldn't break, and the temperature of the arc didn't bother it. And since it wouldn't carry a current, we didn't get the full electrical effect.

"I'm going to convince those birds that this ship is made of something they can't touch! We'll give them a real show!"

He dived downward, back into the battle.

It was a show, all right! It was impossible to fight the Earth ship. The enemy had to concentrate four magnetic rays on it to use their electric weapon, and they could only do that by sheer luck!

And even that was of little use, for they simply lost one of their own ships without harming the *Ancient Mariner* in the least.

Ship after ship crumpled in on itself like crushed tinfoil or hurled itself violently to the ground as the molecular beams touched them. The Satorian fleet was a fleet no longer; it was a small collection of disorganized ships whose commanders had only one thought—to flee!

The few ships that were left spearheaded out into space, using every bit of acceleration that the tough bodies of the Satorians could stand. With a good head start, they were rapidly escaping.

"We can't equal that acceleration," said Wade. "We'll lose them!"

"Nope!" Arcot said grimly. "I want a couple of those ships, and I'm going to get them!"

At four gravities of acceleration, the *Ancient Mariner* drove after the fleeing ships of Sator, but the enemy ships soon dropped rapidly from sight.

Twenty five thousand miles out in space, Arcot cut the acceleration. "We'll catch them now, I think," he said softly. He pushed the little red switch for an instant, then opened it. A moment before, the planet Nansal had been a huge disc behind them. Now it was a tiny thing, a full million miles away.

It took the Satorian fleet over an hour to reach them. They appeared as dim lights in the telectroscope. They rapidly became larger. Arcot had extinguished the lights, and since they were on the sunward side of the approaching ships, the *Ancient Mariner* was effectively invisible.

"They're going to pass us at a pretty good clip," Morey said quietly. "They've been accelerating all this time."

Arcot nodded in agreement. "We'll have to hit them as they come toward us. We'd never get one in passing."

As the ships grew rapidly in the plate, Arcot gave the order to fire!

The molecular rays slashed out toward the onrushing ships, picking them off as fast as the beams could be directed. The rays were invisible in space, so they managed to get several before the Satorians realized what was happening.

Then, in panic, they scattered all over space, fleeing madly from the impossible ship that was firing on them. They knew they had left it behind, yet here it was, waiting for them!

"Let them go," Arcot said. "We've got our specimens, and the rest can carry the word back to Sator that the war is over for them."

It was several hours later that the *Ancient Mariner* approached Nansal again, bringing with it two Satorian ships. By careful use of the heat beam and the molecular beam, the Earthmen had managed to jockey the two battle cruisers back to Nansal.

It was nighttime when they landed. The whole area around the city was illuminated by giant searchlights. Men were working recovering the bodies of the dead, aiding those who had survived, and examining the wreckage.

Arcot settled the two Satorian ships to the ground, and landed the *Ancient Mariner*.

Torlos sprinted over the ground toward them as he saw the great silver ship land. He had been helping in the examination of the wrecked enemy ships.

"Have they attacked anywhere else on the planet?" Arcot asked as he opened the airlock.

Torlos nodded. "They hit five other cities, but they didn't use as big a fleet as they did here. The plan of battle seems to have been for the ships with the new weapons to hit here first and then hit each of the other cities in turn. They didn't have enough to make a full-scale attack; evidently, your presence here made them desperate.

"At any rate, the other cities were able to beat off the magnetic beam ships with the projectors of molecular beams."

"Good," Arcot thought. "Then the Nansal-Sator war is practically over!"

186

XXIII

RICHARD ARCOT stepped into the open airlock of the *Ancient Mariner* and walked down the corridor to the library. There, he found Fuller and Wade battling silently over a game of chess and Morey relaxed in a chair with a book in his hands.

"What a bunch of loafers," Arcot said acidly. "Don't you ever *do* anything?"

"Sure," said Fuller. "The three of us have entered into a lifelong pact with each other to refrain from using a certain weapon which would make this war impossible for all time."

"What war?" Arcot wondered. "And what weapon?"

"This war," Wade grinned, pointing at the chess board. "We have agreed absolutely never to read each other's minds while playing chess."

Morey lowered his book and looked at Arcot. "And just what have you been so busy about?"

"I've been investigating the weapon on board the Satorian ships we captured," Arcot told them. "Quite an interesting effect. The Nansalian scientists and I have been analyzing the equipment for the past three days.

"The Satorians found a way to cut off and direct an electrostatic field. The energy required was tremendous, but they evidently separated the charges on Sator and carried them along on the ships.

"You can see what would happen if a ship were charged negatively and the ship next to it were charged positively!

187

The magnitude of electrostatic forces is terrific! If you put two ounces of iron ions, with a positive charge, on the north pole, and an equivalent amount of chlorine ions, negatively charged, on the south pole, the attraction, even across that distance, would be three hundred and sixty tons!

"They located the negative charges on one ship and the positive charges on the one next to it. Their mutual attraction pulled them toward each other. As they got closer, the charges arced across, heating and fusing the two ships. But they still had enough motion toward each other to crash.

"They were wrecked by less than a tenth of an ounce of ions which were projected to the ship and held there by an automatic field until the ships got close enough to arc through it.

"We still haven't been able to analyze that trick field, though."

"Well, now that we've gotten things straightened out," Fuller said, "let's go home! I'm anxious to leave! We're all ready to go, aren't we?"

Arcot nodded. "All except for one thing. The Supreme Three want to see us. We've got a meeting with them in an hour, so put on your best Sunday pants."

In the Council of Three, Arcot was officially invited to remain with them. The fleet of molecular motion ships was nearing completion—the first one was to roll off the assembly line the next day—but they wanted Arcot, Wade, Morey, and Fuller to remain on Nansal.

"We have a large world here," the Scientist thought at them. "Thanks to you people, we can at last call it our own. We offer you, in the name of the people, your choice of any spot in this world. And we give you—this!" The Scientist came forward. He had a disc-shaped plaque, perhaps three inches in diameter, made of a deep ruby-red metal. In the exact center was a green stone which seemed to shine of its own accord, with a pale, clear, green light; it was transparent and highly refractive. Around it, at the three points of a triangle, were three similar, but smaller stones. Engraved lines ran from each of the stones to the center, and other lines connected the outer three in a triangle. The effect was as though one were looking down at the apex of a regular tetrahedron.

There were characters in Nansalese at each point of the tetrahedron, and other characters engraved in a circle around it.

Arcot turned it in his hand. On the back was a representation of the Nansalian planetary system. The center was a pale yellow, highly-faceted stone which represented the sun. Around this were the orbits of planets, and each of the eleven planets was marked by a different colored stone.

The Scientist was holding in the palm of his hand another such disc, slightly smaller. On it, there were three green stones, one slightly larger than the others.

"This is my badge of office as Scientist of the Three. The stone marked Science is here larger. Your plaque is new. Henceforth, it shall be the Three and a Coordinator!

"Your vote shall outweigh all but a unanimous vote of the Three. To you, this world is answerable, for you have saved our civilization. And when you return, as you have promised, you shall be Coordinator of this system!"

Arcot stood silent for a moment. This was a thing he had never thought of. He was a scientist, and he knew that his ability was limited to that field.

At last, he smiled and replied: "It is a great honor, and it is a great work. But I can not spend my time here always; I must return to my own planet. I can not be fairly in contact with you.

"Therefore, I will make my first move in office now, and suggest that this plaque signify, not the Coordinator, and first power of your country, but Counselor and first friend in all things in which I can serve you.

"The tetrahedron you have chosen; so let it be. The apex is out of the plane of the other points, and I am out of this galaxy. But there is a relationship between the apex and the points of the base, and these lines will exist forever.

"We have been too busy to think of anything else as yet, but our worlds are large, and your worlds are large. Commerce can develop across the ten million light years of space as readily as it now exists across the little space of our own system. It is a journey of but five days, and later machines will make it in less! Commerce will come, and with it will come close communication.

"I will accept this plaque with the understanding that I am but your friend and advisor. Too much power in the hands of one man is bad. Even though you trust me completely, there might be an unscrupulous successor.

"And I must return to my world.

"Your first ship will be ready tomorrow, and when it is completed, my friends and I will leave your planet.

"We will return, though. We are ten million light years apart, but the universe is not to be measured in space anymore, but in time. We are five days apart. I will be nearer to you at all times than is Sator!

"If you wish, others of my race shall come, too. But if you do not want them to come, they will not. I alone have Tharlano's photographs of the route, and I can lose them."

For a moment, the Three spoke together, then the Scientist was again thinking at Arcot.

"Perhaps you are right. It is obvious your people know more than we. They have the molecular ray, and they know no wars; they do not destroy each other. They must be a good race, and we have seen excellent examples in you.

"We can realize your desire to return home, but we ask you to come again. We will remember that you are not ten million light years, but five days, from our planet."

When the conference was ended, Arcot and his friends returned to their ship. Torlos was waiting for them outside the airlock.

"Abaout haow saon you laive?" he asked in English.

"Why—tomorrow," Arcot said, in surprise. "Have you been practicing our language?"

Torlos reverted to telepathy. "Yes, but that is not what

I came to talk to you about. Arcot—can a man of Nansal visit Earth?" Anxiously, hopefully, and hesitatingly, he asked. "I could come back on one of your commercial vessels, or come back when you return. And—and I'm sure I could earn my living on your world! I'm not hard to feed, you know!" He half smiled, but he was too much in earnest to make a perfect success.

Arcot was amazed that he should ask. It was an idea he would very much like to see fulfilled. The idea of metal-boned men with tremendous strength and strange molecular-motion muscles would inspire no friendship, no feeling of kinship, in the people of Earth. But the man himself—a pleasant, kindly, sincere, intelligent giant—would be a far greater argument for the world of Nansal that the most vivid orator would ever be.

Arcot asked the others, and the vote was unanimous—let him come!

The next day, amid great ceremony, the first of the new Nansalian ships came from the factories. When the celebration was over, the four Earthmen and the giant Torlos entered the *Ancient Mariner.*

"Ready to go, Torlos?" Arcot grinned.

"Pearfactly, Ahcut. Tse soonah tse bettah!" he said in his oddly accented English.

Five hours saw them out of the galaxy. Twelve hours more, and they were heading for home at full speed, well out in space.

The Home Galaxy was looming large when they next stopped for observation. Old Tharlano had guided them correctly!

They were going home!

191

Made in the USA
Middletown, DE
17 May 2022

65877099R00113